A Matter of Gravity

A Matter of Gravity

Hélène Vachon

Translated by Phyllis Aronoff and Howard Scott

Talonbooks

Original title: Attraction terrestre
© 2010 Éditions Alto et Hélène Vachon
Translation © 2014 Phyllis Aronoff and Howard Scott

Talonbooks
278 East 1st Avenue, Vancouver, British Columbia, Canada V5T 1A6
www.talonbooks.com

First printing: 2014

Typeset in Filosofia
Printed and bound in Canada on 100% post-consumer recycled paper

Interior and cover design by Typesmith
Cover image: *No One Was Watching*, Dirk Wüstenhagen Imagery, Wuppertal, Germany

Talonbooks gratefully acknowledges the financial support of the Canada Council for the Arts, the Government of Canada through the Canada Book Fund, and the Province of British Columbia through the British Columbia Arts Council and the Book Publishing Tax Credit.

This work was originally published in French as *Attraction terrestre* by Éditions Alto in Quebec City, Quebec, in 2010. We acknowledge the financial support of the Government of Canada, through the National Translation Program, for our translation activities.

Library and Archives Canada Cataloguing in Publication

Vachon, Hélène, 1947–
[Attraction terrestre. English]
    A matter of gravity / Hélène Vachon ; translated by Phyllis Aronoff and Howard Scott.

Translation of: Attraction terrestre.
Issued in print and electronic formats.
ISBN 978-0-88922-840-5 (pbk.).–ISBN 978-0-88922-841-2 (epub)

    I. Aronoff, Phyllis, 1945–, translator II. Scott, Howard, 1952–, translator III. Title. IV. Title: Attraction terrestre. English.

PS8593.A37A9413 2014   C843'.54   C2014-900471-0
                                          C2014-900472-9

There is another world,
but it is in this one.

— Paul Éluard

All joy is revolution. Under the effect of contentment, the face of common *Homo sapiens* changes. From a peaceful state, the platysmas awaken, the zygomaticus major and minor tense, and the orbicularis oris contracts, while the risorius of Santorini retracts the corners of the mouth, which are prime contractile tissue.

This is called smiling, and it's very tiring.

If the source of delight lasts, the smile is transformed into laughter, a veritable *coup d'état* that shakes the entire *Homo sapiens*: the system is energized, the intestines are excited, and the belly, generally so apathetic, suddenly reveals itself to be spasmodic. When the operation has been completed, *Homo sapiens* has lost in lipids what he or she has gained in jubilation and must wait to recover before surrendering to a new fit of gaiety.

Fortunately for *Homo sapiens*, all these contractions then relax. With so much movement, the workers of laughter, smooth or striated, voluntary or involuntary, release into the organism a substance similar to morphine. The shoulders drop, the belly makes peace, and the heart, so misunderstood, slows down. The sphincters remain vigilant, since these rare brief demonstrations of joy in no way dispense them from the obligation to contract absolutely.

~

The man lying in front of me died of laughter. I didn't know such a thing was possible. Hands red, veins blue, sex organ brown, this colourful creature who has been delivered to my care was belching with joy when death took him by surprise.

An abdomen almost as high as it is broad is topped with a round head, a small sphere set directly on a larger one as if the link between them had been forgotten. You immediately sense excess, health squandered. Abuse, pleasure. He doesn't look dead at all. Some people have the good fortune of never looking deceased. No matter what I do, compress his jaw, close his lips, whisper all sorts of noble things in his ear — "Come now, friend, a little decorum, for goodness' sake!" — Risorius ignores it, and the mask becomes even more jolly. So I give in, I always do, I let him have his smile; such opportunities are rare. And I note:

> *Male, 57 years old; 1.69 metres; 78 kilos.*
> *Death: to be confirmed.*

Because I'm waiting, of course. What if his joy was only joy; that is, transient? What if he comes out of it? Spontaneous resurrections are not unheard of, dead people who hesitate and retrace their steps, living ones who act dead. You can't trust anyone anymore.

I wait, therefore I read. One hour, sometimes two. For honour, for the common good. I read; basically, I pray. In the silence of my laboratory, my mouth forms words, whispers, murmurs … They say I'm slow. I'm just a reader. Prudish, patient, I wait. Let death take hold, impose its sounds and its smells, and finally shout at me to get up, close my book, and be done with it once and for all.

End of ceremony.

～

Allow me to introduce myself.

I am a man, forty-six years old. For those who may consider such a description overly brief, I will add only this, since I don't like to talk about myself: I am of average size and fat content; I travel little, preferably on foot; and I have a noisy heart. One last detail, and not the least: I am handsome, but only from the back. As if nature in a tragic moment of distraction got mixed up and confused front and back. One day when I was trying on a suit in a store, I caught sight of myself in the three-way mirror. For a moment, I didn't recognize myself. From the back, I'm quite simply somebody, an observation that is both cheering and sad if you consider that it is impossible to live, as it were, on the wrong side, that there always comes a time when you have to turn around. It is on such occasions that I go to pieces.

I live alone, except for two cats taken in one winter night when I was particularly cold. They walked right in and made themselves at home. I followed them inside, closed the door, and life went on. We respect each other. They let me sleep till four in the morning, when I have to get up to feed them. They take up a lot of space on the bed, and I don't, and in any case I sleep at an angle. But it's awkward for women. I'll come back to women; things don't come easy, it's just something you have to accept, you have no choice. They're there with their bodies around, and it's very disturbing. Not counting the fact that you never know why they like you. Is it for your back? For your front? For your interior? Your exterior? For your upper body? Your lower body? Unless they like all of you, just as you are, without packaging. Anything is possible with them.

Or else it's for the seed. It's priceless these days. With the rain of deaths that's flooding the planet, the loss of productivity that's so depopulating and depressing that they have to clone existing models, I sense a formidable reproductive frenzy among my female associates. I'm an only child and I was never taught to share. The idea of giving up a bit of myself distresses me. We spend our lives scattering ourselves. Sweat, tears, excrement, at a certain point everything deserts you and integrity is sorely tested.

～

The building I live in is inhabited from bottom to top by quiet old things. Everyone here is at least 110 years old.

3

Upstairs from my place is the very old and soundproof Mrs. Le Chevalier. I like her a great deal. She has a certain something that makes you hate anything new. She's so wrinkled and soft-muscled that you have to wonder why no one thought of it before. She knows what I do and accepts me as I am, and our relationship is friendly. She greets me when she meets me, and when I meet her, I also greet her. It's very civilized. My temerity and her longevity have allowed me to develop a kind of dialogue I'm quite proud of, one that's much richer at any rate than the usual *Hello-how-are-you-fine-thank-you*. Think of it: she meets me, I meet her, we greet each other. "How's your health?" I ask bluntly. "Oh, my health!" she replies just as directly. "I'm on the home stretch, you know."

"I don't want to see you for ten years, Mrs. Le Chevalier."

It's so subtle and unexpected. She'll end up on my table, it's inevitable. She's not afraid or anything.

Such an exchange, however, is not without imperfections. All this time I've been saying, "I don't want to see you for ten years," time has been passing, and Mrs. Le Chevalier too will pass. She's not immortal, and that could end up seriously discommoding her. But I hate subtracting, it's not in my nature. Put yourself in my place: "I don't want to see you for nine years, seven months, and four days, Mrs. Le Chevalier." You can't say things like that; she could take it the wrong way.

"Why do you always say the same thing?" she asked me one day.

"Ten years is very elastic," I replied to reassure her.

Downstairs from me, the Boisvert-Dufradels sow terror throughout the neighbourhood. The father and mother work in the environment and recycle everything that moves. They have white teeth, 100 per cent cotton clothes, pleasant expressions, and two very clean little Boisvert-Dufradels who go off to school skipping. It's just not normal. With them, it's forced, they have to look healthy. It's because they have this idea that all's well that ends well and that nothing is lost, nothing is created. It's a bit annoying, because, after all, you just have to look around you to be convinced of the opposite. I don't believe everything can be recycled. There's something irrecoverable in the air.

In short, the Boisvert-Dufradels operate downstairs from me, and it's a miracle they haven't recycled me yet. With the worn look I have quite in spite of myself, I'm afraid a member of their family will one day confuse me with a green bag and rummage around inside me looking for some kind of matter that's still usable. Mrs. Boisvert-Dufradel is particularly zealous at this. I caught her the other day going through the garbage cans of the neighbours to the left, a couple of young lovebirds who are not very conscious about waste recovery — at that age, what's there to recycle, I ask you? She pulled out a whole array of nice old things that were insufficiently worn and were still beautiful despite their age. Mrs. Boisvert-Dufradel was ready and waiting for the couple. Since they're young and sexually active — they're loud and the walls are thin, but the reverse is also true — they sleep. So Mrs. Boisvert-Dufradel had to wait until a quarter after eleven to deliver a stern lecture to them on waste. At a certain point, one of the two birds, the male, I believe, raised a middle finger full of conviction, which put an end to the lady's enthusiasm.

As for my other immediate neighbours, only two are of the male sex. They seldom show themselves and speak little and then usually only out of courtesy. Mr. Hu is a little man who's still vigorous, with ochre skin and dark eyes twinkling with mischief. We get along well, despite the conspiratorial glances he directs at me for no reason whenever we meet, as if we had done great things together that we must keep silent about at all costs.

There isn't much to be said about Mr. Lespérance, my neighbour on the right. He's an old Boy Scout, bald and still straight-backed, who persists, summer and winter, in walking around wearing navy shorts, a white short-sleeved shirt, a red necktie, and a whistle. Far be it from me to reduce Mr. Lespérance to some kind of grotesque image.

Mr. Lespérance must have his depths, like everyone else. But when someone shows his colours so flagrantly, there's a great temptation to rely on appearances, to cut the description short and go on to other things – which is what I'm doing right now.

What can I say about the other tenants? That they exist, that's a fact; that they're no longer young, and that danger is everywhere. Each one of them possesses her own mechanisms of destruction in the short term: Mrs. Le Chevalier forgets to turn off her stove; Mrs. Claire turns on the faucets but doesn't think to turn them off. We've been flooded twice. As for Mrs. Fitzback, strictly speaking, she's not dangerous, but she's one of those people who have a gift for demanding your attention without saying a word. She's always followed by a strong smell of cooked cabbage and a dog that's named Heels because of his tendency to look no farther than the heels of the shoes in front of him. When the shoes stop, he stays there waiting until they are kind enough to start moving again, which he then does himself with great patience and resignation. When Mrs. Fitzback is too tired or the weather is threatening, I make it my duty to take Heels out, an act of altruism that is totally unjustified – the lady has sufficient ballast to withstand hurricanes, maelstroms, tornadoes, and other disturbances. To thank me, Mrs. Fitzback gives me one of her immaculate smiles that plunge me into a state of perplexity close to distress, a laborious, complicated gymnastic exercise whose purpose is less to express joy than to keep in place the curious amphitheatre of false ivory erected in her mouth.

I won't mention all the other tenants, who go on living without the means to do so, and their lapses of memory and awkward moments. I systematically check the building, I take dogs out, I turn taps and stoves off; sometimes I turn dogs off and take stoves out. I try to anticipate, but you can't anticipate everything.

That's it for the immediate environment and the general feminine climate. Because in spite of Hu, the Scout, and the protesting middle finger, the building has a very clear preference for the *anima*. That's okay with me, but my *animus* gets bored sometimes. And he's not the only one. The *animas* get bored too, I see it clearly in their stooped backs, their bobbling heads, their way of talking to themselves. Even past the age of one hundred, it isn't normal to find yourself with such a huge deficit of the other sex. The ratio is twelve women to one man. Everybody loses by it. Not to mention balance. More women have to pass on or more men stay on; that is, more women and men have to pass on and stay on at the same time. If not, they can't exist side by side, and the dialogue is interrupted, it's an eternal station platform.

But there isn't just the building. I should warn you, we won't be alone. The world is wide and I have horizons. There are a lot of people. A certain number of dead people – a lot of us are dying, it's a massacre – others living. There's Clotilde, who I've been trying to break up with for quite a while without the least success; there's my mother; and there's my father, dead but very present, who persisted all his life in doing the opposite of what I do; there are Julian, Alfred, Zita, and other people, too – more or less temporary, more or less characters, but whose names I won't reveal out of tact – and finally, the cats I've already referred to, small and furry, but that's no reason not to mention them. If we refused to speak of anything small and furry, what would we talk about? Take, for instance, that hairy little doctor who saw me on Christmas Eve without for a second suspecting that he too was part of the scenery and contributed to the jovial atmosphere that's just waiting to blossom in every one of us.

1

The contractions began on Christmas Eve. Around six o'clock, my heart started pounding and I had to reconcile myself to breathing through my mouth, which hadn't occurred for a long time. My first thought was for my mother, who all my life has claimed that my heart doesn't work right. My second thought was for my heart: it's true that it doesn't work right, but the problem isn't with the organ. The problem lies elsewhere. Despite the power of gravity the earth exercises, there's a permanent little cushion of air between it and me that, besides making me look tall, causes me all kinds of problems, not the least of which is the chronic instability marking my human relationships. Being faced with someone who's constantly wavering, who's floating somewhere between heaven and earth with no apparent desire to come to rest, is enough to discourage people with the best of intentions, and I can only admire the tenacity of those who persevere, who are not put off either by my propensity or my real desire to be elsewhere.

At a certain point, inhaling through my mouth no longer sufficed, and I started panting, making the characteristic whistle of the asthmatic on the verge of catalepsy (*siiiiiiiii* …). Thinking that I was calling him for a brushing, Sully immediately came running with his coat begging. I rushed to the emergency room of the nearest hospital, dreading that they'd make me spend the night there. The prospect was all the less inviting because I had decided to distinguish myself from my peers by spending Christmas Eve alone quietly reading for a few hours before going to bed in the brand new pyjamas I had bought for the occasion.

The wait lasted a little less than three hours and nine minutes. Fortunately, I had thought to bring a book, essential equipment for survival in the forest. Starting a book is always a trial, and the first pages are difficult. It is therefore recommended that you do it in a hospital. A total stranger addresses you in all his innocence, his naivety, his pretensions, and right away you're supposed to like him. Hold on! Not so fast, my friend! I always read the first few pages with huge reservations, holding the book far from me, predisposed as I am against anything I can't immediately relate to myself – that is, almost everything. The first thirty pages are the worst. What are they talking about? Where is the action taking place and in what time period? Good God, what is happening? After that, you give up on it or it keeps going by itself. So it had already been quite a while since I had finished the book, we'd had lots of time to get acquainted, to connect, to disconnect, and we were saying our goodbyes on the station platform when I heard Number 17 called. I knew it was me right away and I leapt to my feet as if I were late.

An ethereal white nurse – the kind of woman every man dreams of running into at least once a day, the timeless type that raises very little dust – was standing in front of me activating her little zygomaticus. There was an immediate, fleeting encounter between us, a mutual recognition of a shared trait, a salutary and sanitary emptiness between the earth and the body. No matter what men do, none will ever achieve such a degree of non-existence.

"The doctor is waiting for you."

I took a step into the room indicated, but there didn't seem to be much point. The doctor in question was ensconced in his rolling chair, offering his back to me. His front was occupied elsewhere, drawn more by the images scrolling on his computer screen than by my own concrete existence. I took another step forward and felt a pressing need to introduce myself.

"Here I am, sir. Number 17."

He didn't stand up or anything. His back remained impassive, his entire human person bent resolutely toward the screen, and if it hadn't been for my heart taking off again at a flat-out gallop, I might have believed I didn't exist. No matter what they say, a beating heart is still the best sign of life there is, especially in a hospital.

"Hermann, male, residing at 72 des Échelles Street, that's you," the doctor pronounced. His voice was low, a kind of slightly nasal head tone.

"Pleased to meet you," I said.

Then he did something extraordinary: he turned and looked at me, with his nose, his mouth, and his entire human person. A torso pivoting on casters is beautiful. I let my joy burst forth, I couldn't help myself.

"You must be awfully happy to be able to put a face to the words!"

Since he didn't appear to understand, I thought I should add: "It's the concrete over the abstract, and it's not every day you have something to celebrate."

I detected in him none of the signs of rejoicing you would rightfully expect in one human being meeting another. I made one final and ultimate attempt: "We have both just escaped from the grip of the virtual. I think that deserves to be celebrated."

I'm like that, I like to take the time to make a person's acquaintance, individually, or else what's the point of being unique?

Since the doctor couldn't be bothered to ask me to take a seat, I went and sat down in front of him. He was the worst of all things: neither handsome nor ugly, neither fat nor thin, nothing to hold your attention, interrupted movements; in short, an incomplete creature in every respect.

"My heart is skipping beats," I said to put him at ease.

"Just the heart, are you sure?"

"It makes a big jump, two little ones, and then – the big leap …"

"Sit down."

"I'm sitting."

"Ah! The big leap?"

"The big leap, yes. Into the void."

He nodded.

"It's contracting abnormally, I'm sure of it. Even my cats have noticed it. Instead of going *baboom! baboom!* like everybody else's, it goes *booooom dash baboom*."

"Are you perspiring a lot?"

"Right now?"

"In general."

"I don't perspire in general."

"And sleep?"

"Not that I know of."

"Could you be more clear?"

"I sleep in segments."

"Your thyroid is enlarged. It shows in your eyes. Your cats saw that too, perhaps?"

"They didn't want to worry me, I imagine."

"Its volume has nearly doubled, I'd say."

"These days, you know, I don't mind a little swelling."

"I'm not joking, sir."

He stood up and came over to me, and I felt my thyroid gland retreat behind my Adam's apple. My gland is shy, and I'm the only one who can get near it.

"*Hyperactive* would be the word," said the doctor after feeling it. He sat down heavily in his chair. "Why do you keep moving all the time?"

"It's because of the cushion. It's a long story. I'm here without being here, do you understand? I waver and waver, you have no idea. I'm expected on the right, I'm on the left; one day I'm here, the next, not; that's the way it is."

"You also have a funny odour."

"It's an occupational hazard, sir. The air cushion doesn't block it completely. With all the dead people that rain down on me every day."

"And what is it that you do every day?"

"I embalm, sir. In every sense of the word."

"Ah!"

"That's what I say too."

He paused pensively.

"I'm also short of breath," I said, to encourage him to continue. "Generally speaking, I'm short of breath."

"Of course."

"And not only because of the formaldehyde. Just the idea that I could be short of oxygen one day is unbearable to me."

He scribbled something about something. I sighed.

"Have you ever considered the fact that, above five thousand feet, oxygen becomes rarefied? I'm purposely expressing myself in feet – in metres, I would already be dead."

"What do you need with five thousand feet?"

"We all need more. Man needs a lot more than he imagines; he occupies a space infinitely larger than the volume of his body. It's a misconception that ..."

"You're suffering from anxiety, sir."

"I believe you."

"It's a normal phenomenon in an older person, especially one who's solitary."

"What makes you think I'm an older person?"

A limpid silence.

"I'm a lot younger than that, you know. Under this austere exterior, I admit, I'm only forty-six."

"That's hard to believe."

"And what makes you think I'm alone?"

"If you only knew how many poor wretches end up in the hospital on Christmas Eve!"

"I don't like that idea at all."

"I'm sorry."

"You could have picked another day."

"You're the one who came here, may I remind you."

"And I'm not alone. I'm in a relationship, well, sort of a relationship. Clotilde is an absolutely charming woman. Unfortunately there's Zita, a lot more supple and ..."

He stood up, indicating the clock – a big round thing flat as a pancake – and the troop of poor wretches waiting their turns, and went to the door. I deduced that he was cutting me off, and I cut myself off. I hate words that hang in the air, just hang there without anyone catching them. It's air pollution and it heats up the greenhouse effect. He handed me a slip of paper that was perfectly legible and left me there, advising me to enjoy myself a little.

On the way home, I didn't encounter another living soul, nor a single open pharmacy. It's really not possible that everyone is having fun on Christmas Eve! I went to bed in a foul mood with my cats around me, my hand clutching my new pyjamas right where my heart was contracting even more, asking myself how on earth I had achieved the feat of spoiling the evening after going to so much trouble to convince Clotilde that it was better to go to bed early so as to be in good shape the next day.

2

No, not everybody is having fun on Christmas Eve, especially not that big strapping guy sitting next to Hermann in the hospital waiting room. Endowed with an above-average build, he could easily occupy two chairs if he didn't make it a point of honour, in all circumstances but particularly in public places, to occupy only one, an exploit he accomplishes only at the cost of constant compression, which obliges him to stand up frequently to allow his heart to pump blood properly through the thousand and one vessels that are supposed to irrigate his body.

He hasn't been called yet, and for good reason: he has Number 32, and they've just called 12, a scrawny little fellow bent over a cane that's almost as unsteady as he is. The man sighs, waits, looks at the others. He'd practise his scales if he weren't afraid of frightening the twenty other people who are waiting. At first glance, it can be surprising to see a person running ten fingers over his knees, especially in a practically full waiting room, where the least quiver is like an uprising. Is it the lighting, is it the confined space? Everything seems too close, too crowded. There's not enough distance between the chairs, and the aisles are too narrow. He stands up, takes a few steps, swings his arms, massages his calves, straightens up again. How can they be so motionless on Christmas Eve? he wonders oddly. His eyes move from one to another without sympathy. Any human gathering is in itself disturbing, if not to say depressing. Why is that? It's as if the sample represented the whole, so that everything is a bit flat, homogeneous, and rather ugly. A fat lady dozes, mouth open (this is the lot of elderly sleepers), knees hanging open onto emptiness; a child sleeps, mouth agape (this is the lot of young sleepers with colds), ready to receive the thick flow of yellow snot that hesitates for a moment on the edge of the protruding lip, then valiantly overcomes the obstacle and returns to its source, slipping into the mouth and into the stomach to be digested and expelled in another form. Nothing is lost, thinks the big man. There's something fascinating about it.

Beside him, Number 17 reads without pause, with a totally childlike absorption, giving each page equal attention, twenty-six seconds for each one, the man calculates. How is this possible? Normally, people don't read that way. A normal reader pauses, looks up, breathes in, breathes out. Not Number 17. This absolute concentration surprises him and then annoys him. He stands up again, stirs up the air enough to fully oxygenate the whole waiting room, but it's no use, the little exercise continues, page after page, twenty-six seconds, as if each one deserved equal attention. A bionic reader, thinks the man.

He is here for his hands. Three weeks ago, he came to the hospital because his hands were in a pitiful state. With age, they have grown even wider and the palms have become deeper in the middle, pushing the dense flesh to the sides, which makes them look like two big soft pancakes. The fingers are short, wide at the base and then tapering, but just a little. It's a miracle they don't get stuck when they press the keys. There are shooting pains in the index and middle fingers of his right hand. He has tried massaging them, it doesn't help. The index finger has become misshapen at the third phalanx – it has shifted to the left as if it wanted nothing to do with the other fingers – while the middle finger has gradually gotten thicker, with a kind of knot at the swollen second phalanx. Thirty years devoted exclusively to music, to using ten fingers all day long, and it's come to this.

Across from him, a pretty girl with a bandage on her forehead is leafing through a fashion magazine, scratching her left calf. With the bandage around her forehead – a tiny spot of blood has seeped through the gauze – her slightly long, hooked nose and her dark complexion, she almost looks like an Indian. Without the red lipstick that gives her a big shiny mouth, of course, and that grey pullover that reveals her bra and the compressed flesh spilling out of it. The man observes her for a moment without forming a precise idea of what she represents to him. Does he find her beautiful? Attractive? How can he know? God, everything is so complicated! He imagines himself with her, at least he tries to, but it isn't convincing or it's ridiculous.

His comings and goings have woken up the snot-nosed kid, who is now running around the empty chairs and then falling on its mother's knees with cries of joy. A long string of drool? snot? mucus? — the secretions are accumulating inexorably — hangs from the child's mouth, trembling with its movements and landing in the woolly folds of its mother's skirt.

Frail Number 12 with the cane has just left the consulting room and is walking slowly toward the exit. Outside, the wind swirls the snow, creating the impression that it is rising rather than falling. That would be good, thinks the man. For once, just for once.

The toddler trips on a chair and falls. Its expression goes from astonishment to questioning. No one has seen; its honour is intact. The child gets up and starts again. The girl with the bandage has finished reading her magazine. She has wedged card Number 27 under her right thigh, with only the upper half of the 2 and 7 still visible. She reaches for another magazine and intercepts the gaze of the man who is staring at her. Her black hair is gathered in a smooth, shiny ponytail.

He looks at the girl's hands. He finds their pudgy, milky whiteness a bit repellent. The hands don't go with the brown face. He doesn't like this kind of contrast, tanned face and white flesh, blonde hair and black pubic hair, the inconsistency of bodies is disagreeable to him. Her fingernails are endless and are lacquered in shiny purple, and her fingers are adorned with half a dozen rings. The man shakes his head. That won't do, he says to himself, that's not it at all. He exhales, pushing the air noisily out of his lungs. Time does not pass. The man sighs. In his hand, card Number 32 is moist.

And then they call Number 17, the disquieting bionic reader, who, after a long adoring look at the pale nurse, leaps to his feet and dashes to the consulting room. Full silhouette, nondescript, stooped shoulders that you imagine permanently bent over something or someone – but who? – hair growing low on the neck, ending in a thin brown brush that sneaks under his collar. That's the treasure, thinks the man, the thing that's touching about him, that pale strand of silky hair, and those hands that were just now making the pages flutter. The hands had looked to him like the purest, most noble expression of vital energy. Golden-brown skin covered with a pale down that must gleam when, by some happy chance, the sun graces it with a ray, clean shiny fingernails, little oases of light trimmed short for cleanliness. And then the palm. Curved, large enough to hold a fruit, supple enough to mould itself to any object.

All of a sudden, the toddler heads for him. A wet, almost sensual smile on its lips, it leaves its mother's knees and rushes forward in an assault on his. The man stiffens abruptly in a state of expectant, potentially painful passivity. The child gives him a long look. What do I look like from down there? wonders Number 32. Prominent chin, large jaw, deep nostrils protected by a thicket of hair. Along with the drool, a bunch of inarticulate sounds gush from the child's mouth. The man doesn't understand. His ear has never been exposed to children's babble. The only responses that come to him are the ones generally used in society: "I beg your pardon?" or "What did you say?" but those aren't the questions to ask and in any case that's not the way to talk to a child. His frozen mask stiffens even more, while his large body, his massive thighs, his rigid back, remain at attention. Moving would cause the child to fall, moving would bring the mother's condemnation upon him. And while the child's moist, sticky hands find a solid support and an unanticipated playground in the broad surface of his knees, the big man waits for it all to end, for the mother to finally summon her son back or for his number to be called. His pants are already stained, the little hands are busy untangling a wet string of drool, an inextricable jumble of knots. That's life, the man repeats to himself, turning his head toward the counter, sighing. Number 17 hasn't come out yet.

Instinctively, the man has hidden his hands from view. He has no desire for the child to notice them and react with incomprehension, so he's tucked them under his knees, between his warm thighs.

Number 17 leaves the consulting room and then the hospital. The man's eyes follow him for a moment. Number 18 – how predictable it all is, he thinks – should get up and go sit down in front of a doctor the man imagines to be somewhat rushed. An old woman leans over to her companion and whispers something in his ear. He's Number 18. She grabs his arm and tries unsuccessfully to raise him, asks him to stand, come on, get up, it's our turn, we mustn't keep the doctor waiting. The old man finally agrees to get himself in gear, but it takes forever.

Let's use this time that's dragging on to take a quick look back and try to understand, if we ever can, that character, that Number 32, the prisoner of the snot-nosed toddler who's slumped on him – it's David and Goliath, no less – who has no hope of standing up, jumping, and getting the blood circulating in his legs. Let's go back forty-one years, to the month of August, the nineteenth, to be precise. It's 11:47 a.m. Number 32 is being born. Forgetting the advice of the nurse, the mother inhales and exhales erratically, and finally expels a fetus of impressive dimensions, which the father receives, almost drops, and prevents from falling only by dint of an effort he will later describe as superhuman.

August 19 was marked with a red *X* by his parents. The event was worth celebrating, not only because of the size of the infant but because they had been trying for years to have a baby, to the point that they sometimes wondered if they had missed an entire section of the instruction manual. And because it was the first time they had procreated and they had never had a chance to experience normality, they gazed timidly at their child, filled with doubt and a vague feeling of disapproval. If someone could have told them that from this compact, placid mass, this disturbing combination of heavy limbs, thick joints, and connections indiscernible under the fat, there would spring forth a pianist of renown, the course of their lives – and especially that of their son – might have been changed.

They experienced the early days of the child's life in a state of almost perpetual astonishment, the father especially, who started to cast a suspicious eye on the mother. How could such a delicate little creature have produced a specimen of such dimensions? And how could he, just as delicate a creature (but undeniably masculine), have contributed to such a conception? He had even wondered if their light builds were not incompatible with an action as mundane, as carnal as procreation. Faced with the painful proof that the child could only have come from his wife (he had attended the birth with his eyes closed, but still), he had to wonder about the other gene carrier; that is, himself. There's simply no way I could have made that, he repeated to himself while his eyes stoically surveyed the long, broad expanse of the child.

But there was something even more serious: the external appearance of the father, the almost spider-like delicacy of his frame, was nothing compared to his immoderate love of all things subtle and ethereal – he was an expert in Byzantine and Persian miniatures – and his disdain, which was equally immoderate, for things in large sizes. In deciding to perpetuate his line, he had expected more, or rather, less, a lot less – a child whose proportions were more human or were based more on his own. In his worst moments of doubt, he told himself that with all those failed attempts to create a successor, he and his wife had forced the hand of destiny. What becomes of unused seed? It must have been stored somewhere, in some hidden recess in his wife, and, fruitless attempt after fruitless attempt, accumulated inexorably. A single spermatozoon could not have done all that by itself. Lurking in the shadows, the contingent of unrequisitioned gametes had bided their time until the long-awaited moment of fertilization, to charge after the victorious spermatozoon and assail the poor ovum like a gang of thugs swooping down on their prey. We overdid it, he repeated to himself. We shouldn't have. And now, here I am, stuck with a child who is unlike me in every way, who has neither my hands nor my eyes nor my build.

The oafish child grew in length and breadth without the least sign of stabilizing. Year after year, he gained more weight and took up more space in the house. Especially after the acquisition of the famous Schimmel baby grand, a piano with a resonant bass, which had been purchased after years of guilt – and because of the boy's relentless (and sometimes damaging) assaults on any pianos that had the misfortune to be found in his path.

At what point did the father give up trying to understand? He himself would not have been able to say. Losing interest in the question, he also lost interest in the child. He immersed himself body and soul in the study of miniatures again, scoured the world and its museums in search of rare specimens and created his own collection, which he protected from light (and even from noise!) with maniacal care, his greatest concern being to keep away his big lout of a son who, overjoyed at seeing his father, would throw himself at him at every opportunity, clamouring for bread and circuses. The day the lad with one swipe of his left hand (sheer clumsiness!) decapitated a tin-alloy miniature fifty-two millimetres high depicting a seated marchioness in evening dress (she unfortunately was matched with a standing marquis), the father transported the entire collection to a furnished apartment he rented, where he ended up living permanently. This allowed him to kill two birds with one stone: to save his collection of precious objects and to end all carnal relations with his wife.

His wife did not have time to form an accurate idea of her son's talent; in any case, she did not witness his success. She died at thirty-nine, crippled with rheumatism, loneliness, and melancholy. The father travelled all the more, returning and leaving again, spacing his visits home further and further apart, writing less and less, his pen faltering, his eyes raised to the sky, waiting for the right word or for a circumlocution that might at least allow him to keep up appearances. The son also travelled, playing more and more concerts and tours, returning and leaving again, writing each time his father wrote, his pen faltering, his eyes on his big hands, waiting for the right turn of phrase that might at least allow *him* to keep up appearances.

The words were never right; at any rate, appearances were not kept up. The correspondence petered out. The father gave up a second time, citing self-deception: a pianist with huge paws and fingers as fat as sausages could not expect to have a very long career. So as not to have to console him when the fall came, he refrained from congratulating the son when a new record came out or when, by a huge coincidence, he came across an article praising the "solidly built artist the subtlety of whose playing is a pleasant surprise, like fine embroidery coming from the hands of an *Anthropopithecus*."

Having not long of a mother and not much of a father leaves marks, it seems. If you add unheard-of proportions and more than ordinary gifts for animal life, the life that beats, moves, and is drawn toward fellow beings, you get this Number 32, a larger-than-life forty-one-year-old, too tall, too fat, with prematurely aged fingers and a compromised musical career. He's here this evening to get the results of the tests that have been carried out on his person. And because he doesn't want to be alone on Christmas Eve.

He hadn't liked it one bit. Three weeks earlier, he had sat down in front of the doctor and held out his two hands like two unwieldy objects he wanted to be rid of for a while. The doctor had barely looked at them. Weary of the usual rhinitises and sinusitises of the season, he had looked the man up and down and from side to side before launching his assault on the mountain of white flesh. It might be an opportunity not to be missed, the doctor had thought. Under this placid collection of organs and limbs, there might be new germs, unknown bacteria, portents of equally unknown diseases that he, an unfulfilled doctor of fifty-two, would help shed light on. Everything was scrutinized: head, neck, arms, abdomen, legs, ankles, feet, and so on. The big man submitted, forcing himself to remain passive but unable not to feel embarrassed – he hadn't showered, certain that the precaution was unnecessary. It's just a difficult few minutes to get through, he told himself silently, while the expert hands explored his back, his belly, his throat. He had to accept being touched and palpated, even like that, even in passing, to surrender himself to others for once, to give up not just ten fingers but his entire body with its solid surfaces, its never-explored hollows, its sensitive zones, its furrows, its folds. He had to accept it. He had to. You cannot live indefinitely in silence and reclusion, there have to be pauses, times when you leave your burrow to contemplate the sky, head back and arms wide open. He had hated the experience.

Slumped over his knees, the child is still playing. Number 30 has just disappeared behind the doctor's door. The girl with the bandage is gone. The man sighs. He doesn't have much longer to wait. He's eager to stand up, but he doesn't. His patience is infinite; it's Christmas and no one is waiting for him.

And then, finally, he's the one being called. He prepares to get up, tall, stout, out of breath, hobbled. The child is still clinging to his knee. He has to remove the slippery little suckers one by one, but the child has no intention of letting go; it hangs on and stiffens. Second call for Number 32. The man gives the mother a desperate look, and she returns the look with one that's placid, indifferent. The man will have to tear himself away and escape, which he does in a final burst of energy, his forehead crimson, with a feeling of rending living tissue. The child, having lost its support, its warm, solid haven, falls on its back and starts to cry.

3

When I opened my eyes the next day after a night as fleeting as it was short, the contrast between the evening I had expected and the one I actually spent struck me. So did my two cats, but it was no time for fun and games. I buried my head under the sheets, imploring the heavens to let me sink into oblivion. The cats had no intention of allowing that. The cat food was still sitting on the kitchen counter and they refused to wait any longer to stuff their faces. It's not Christmas every day and they can read a calendar as well as anyone.

Clotilde phoned at eleven, obviously rested and bursting with energy, a description that in her case is rather redundant. Clotilde is short and rosy-cheeked, even-tempered and ready for anything, for love or any other activity; in short, the complete opposite of me. Why am I with her? I don't know. One fine morning, we simply woke up together and, with the help of the cushion, I thought things could be like that until the end of time.

"Is this the time we wake up?" cooed Clotilde.

The telephone cord immediately curled up, and so did I. I hate this kind of opening, which has something patronizing and totally childish about it.

"I hardly closed my eyes," I growled. "Not one of them. Clotilde, if you don't mind, we …"

"No way, my pet! I'll meet you at the café. My treat."

I closed my eyes after an envious glance at the cats, sated and performing their ablutions at the foot of the bed.

"Maybe just a little nap …"

"No. If you haven't slept, as you say, it's too late now."

Clotilde has a soft spot for the local café because that's where we met and because they let her exhibit some of her creations, stuffed birds that are not always identifiable but that sell well.

Before leaving the apartment, I called my mother.

"Is that you, Champ?"

I hate this opening almost as much as the other one. I don't know why my mother persists in sticking me with that ridiculous nickname.

"Mom …"

"I was wondering when you were going to call. I didn't want to wake you. You shouldn't wake up lovebirds on Christmas morning, isn't that so?"

Lovebirds?

"Mom …"

"Do you like her at least?"

"Meaning …?"

"Don't tell me you don't have anybody yet …"

"Meaning …?"

"Stop saying *Meaning?* okay?"

Silence.

"I wouldn't want …" my mother began again.

If we kept leaving our sentences unfinished, we'd be headed straight for a dialogue, which is to be avoided on Christmas Day.

"What wouldn't you want, Mom?"

I heard a long, very long, sigh.

"I wouldn't want you to spend the rest of your life alone."

"I'm not alone."

She gave a kind of sad laugh. "The cats …"

"Yes, the cats."

"That's not somebody."

"Of course it is."

"And one day they'll die."

"So will I, Mom."

"And so will I," she added in a lower voice.

I clutched the receiver tighter. "Are you having problems?"

"Not that I know of. But I wonder what an old woman like me is still doing on this earth."

I felt my throat tighten.

"What's stopping you, Hermann?"

"Stopping me from what?"

"From having a more ... normal life?"

Normal? I scanned the room looking for the meaning, but the scoundrel was hiding.

"You're so quick, so active, so decisive ..." continued my mother.

"What?!"

"Just like me."

"Mom ..."

"Yes, Champ?"

"Last night, I felt something weird ..."

"Something weird? I hope so, Champ. If you don't feel it at your age, when will you?"

She had recovered completely.

"I'm hanging up now."

"Already?" said my mother.

"I'm meeting someone."

Silence.

"Well then, merry Christmas, my son."

My son. It was so unexpected that I didn't know what to say.

"Hermann? Are you there, Hermann?"

"I'm here."

Another silence. My mother was breathing at the other end of the line. "You're well, at least?"

"I'm fine. Merry Christmas, Mom."

I hung up and clamped my hand over my mouth to keep all that damn liquid from coming out. I never do anything like other people. When I'm about to cry, the tears fill my mouth first. A warm, salty tide floods my throat before it goes up to my eyes. Nine times out of ten, I manage to dam the flow well before the fateful move upward, which means that my eyes are (almost) always dry.

Clotilde was waiting for me at the café, pink, perky, and totally caring. Other than her, a couple with kids, and a fat man at the table in the back, the place was empty. I sank down into a banquette. There was an enormous bouquet of white carnations in the middle of the table.

"I don't know what's the matter with me ..." I began.

Clotilde looked into my eyes, her face serious. Her complexion even paled. At least that's what it seemed like to me. She was wearing a severe black suit, brightened only by a series of miniature birds proudly spreading their wings, which were covered with red and green sequins.

"You've got a long face, old man!"

It must have been the *old man* that triggered it. You don't call the love of your life *old man*, and the change of perspective revived my hope that she didn't love me as much as she thought. I'm an incorrigible optimist.

"What the heck am I doing here?" I muttered.

Clotilde squeezed my arm.

"You've come to have breakfast with me on Christmas morning in a café we like. What's so terrible about that?"

I got up without warning and ran to the washroom. I splashed icy water on my face until my skin was as red as Clotilde's and blew my nose several times. I returned to my seat across from Clotilde, who was waiting for me without seeming overly concerned, as if I had just stepped out to make a phone call.

"Clotilde ..."

"Yes?"

"I don't deserve you."

My God, that was dumb! And so trite. I was easily worthy of her, we both knew it.

"No," said Clotilde, unruffled.

"But I'm leaving."

Clotilde didn't bat an eye. She looked at me, shrugged her

shoulders in a movement that was both nonchalant and graceful, and went back to eating. If she hadn't speared her croissant with her fork, which she wasn't in the habit of doing, I might have believed that nothing had happened.

"That's a fixation of yours!"

"I need to step back a bit," I stammered. Another cliché, when I should have brought out the arsenal of original expressions to appeal to her feelings.

"Is there someone else?"

Yes, there was someone else. There was Zita, with her soul and her openness, Zita so alive, so painfully absent, in her multipocket jumpsuit. Yes, there was someone else, but that someone else didn't know it.

"Sort of."

Clotilde wiped her mouth with her napkin, first one corner, then the other.

"It's absolutely out of the question," she said with surprising assurance.

You don't break up with Clotilde, you give in. There are some people who capitulate in the face of adversity. You blow on them and they buckle. Not Clotilde. Clotilde is one of those people who have presence, who are so there that it's impossible to disregard them. I'd like to believe they're sent to us by the gods to compensate for our ditherings, our shameful indecisiveness. But to tell the truth, I'm not sure.

Clotilde stood up, pushed her chair in under the table in that careful way she has, which I call her sensitivity toward inanimate objects, put on her heavy coat (without my help, or I would remember), and left the restaurant with a quick nod to the sole waiter on duty that day.

～

When I returned home the second time that Christmas morning, the apartment still seemed full of Clotilde. Knick-knacks, kitchenware, little bottles, not to mention clothes still permeated with her smell, and stuffed birds scattered here and there in the living room, bedroom, and bathroom. I was sitting in an armchair we'd bought together, I was reading a book she'd loaned me, the flowers on the table were still fresh. I don't buy many flowers, because of the funeral parlour smell they trail everywhere. What obscure instinct had led her, day after day, to accumulate so many tangible signs of her presence in my apartment?

I don't know how much time passed. The sick feeling of the day before came back and I gasped for air several times like a fish taken out of its bowl. I got up and ran to the café. The remains of breakfast were still there. I went to the table and sat down at Clotilde's place, staring stupidly at the crumbs of croissant and the ring of coffee at the bottom of her cup.

A few minutes later, I began to clear the table, mechanically piling cups, saucers, and plates as I was in the habit of doing when we ate at my place. It was only when the waiter came over looking surprised that I realized what I was doing. I turned on my heel and left the café, stammering trite apologies.

The trouble with me is that I never know whether my life is funny or sad. I don't know how to separate the serious from the trivial or the comical. How often have I smiled when it was a time for solemnity or had a lump in my throat when everyone else chose to laugh?

4

Number 32's Christmas Eve appointment, his second one with the hairy doctor, was decisive. When he learned, in quick succession, that he was suffering from progressive rheumatoid arthritis, emphysema, and early Parkinson's, he understood that his career as a musician was not just threatened by a twisted index finger and knotted phalanges, but was, so to speak, moribund.

"It's a lot for just one body," mumbled the doctor, who had never been able to offer more than a few simple and usually evasive words of sympathy. "A lot ..." he added, nevertheless with touching conviction.

He stood there, arms dangling, and continued to look the sad fellow slumped in front of him up and down and left to right, tracing a cross, as if it were inconceivable that this large body could be apprehended in a single glance.

The large body in question was, at that particular moment, devastated. Destroyed, in five complicated scientific words, including a disturbing adjective and a proper noun that didn't mean much to him other than that Parkinson must have been the sad fellow who had once trembled and had given his name to that tremor. Progressive. Rheumatoid. Arthritis. Emphysema. Parkinson's.

"Let's begin at the beginning ..." Number 32 stammered.

The doctor's only answer was to go to the wall where a set of X-rays showed two enormous lobes shaped like walnuts, amputated from their base for lack of space on the film.

"Those are my lungs?"

"Obviously. What else would they be?"

"Obviously," the man replied. "The kidneys are smaller, they would fit on the X-ray, I imagine."

Although he hated seeing himself in photographs, he forced himself to look. He was not and never had been photogenic, and even his lungs were loath to lend themselves to comparison. While he kept telling himself they weren't visible, that only this little runt of a doctor had seen them, he didn't at all like the look of those bloated walnuts with their misshapen contours.

"Your lungs are in bad shape. If you continue at this rate, your chances aren't very good."

"How can you tell they're in bad shape?"

"From your air sacs. Your alveoli. Or if you prefer, your pulmonary interstitial spaces."

"I prefer air sacs."

"I'm not joking, sir."

Another look at the X-rays. The doctor pointed an accusatory finger at the nut on the left. "Too big. Much too big."

"Normal," Number 32 felt he should point out. "Everything with me is too big or too fat."

"The tissues have already lost a good deal of their elasticity, the sacs can no longer inflate and deflate as they should."

"I'm sorry."

"In short, you're well on the way to emphysema."

A rather painful silence followed. The man's breathing took the opportunity to make itself heard, to grow louder in the narrow space of unoccupied time, a sort of plaintive hissing, certainly nothing that normal lungs couldn't accommodate.

"I'm only forty-one," he suddenly declared as if that were a reason to redo the tests from the start.

"It's hard to believe," the doctor replied.

"I'll never have the time ..."

The doctor sighed and looked down at the floor. He should have asked: "The time for what?" But no. Asking the question would parachute him right into the man's private life, and if there was one thing he avoided, it was being parachuted into a person's private life.

"I'm going to end up suffocating, is that it?"

The doctor shook his head, half yes, half no. "Are you perspiring a lot?"

"Right now?"

"In general."

"Not that I know of."

"And sleep?"

"What about sleep?"

"Do you sleep?"

"In general?"

The doctor made an impatient gesture. "In general, yes. Not right now, you're not sleeping now, you'd know it and so would I."

"I sleep. In the daytime especially."

"Do you work at night?"

"I work when I can, I work when I'm awake."

"Do your hands always tremble like that?"

"Alcohol, perhaps. Maybe I drink too much."

"It's not alcohol."

An angel passed, an ethereal white nurse tiptoeing in to get a file. As she closed the door, she turned to Number 32 and smiled at him, the kind of smile that could make the tiniest air sacs swell.

"Did you drink before coming here?"

"No," he answered, thinking yes, maybe.

"Because there's worse, it's my duty to tell you."

"My lungs are done for. What could be worse than lungs that are done for?"

"A brain that's done for," declared the doctor, straightening up, as if he were making a solemn declaration.

"My brain isn't doing too badly."

"Your right hand ..."

"What about my right hand?"

"It trembles. I saw it when you came the other day, but I didn't want to worry you before I was certain."

"What are you trying to tell me?"

"That you have another illness."

Silence.

"Is the first one not valid anymore? What do we do with the engorged alveoli? The sacs that don't inflate and deflate properly?"

"They're secondary. For the time being. The tests have revealed a more serious problem. A problem located precisely in the motor control area."

The man took a deep breath. "Could you be more clear? To me, *motor control* makes me think of a car."

"You're suffering from a serious dopamine imbalance. In other words, certain cells in your brain, the ones that are supposed to secrete dopamine, to be precise, can no longer do so properly."

"Why not?"

"Because they're dying, sir. I'm sorry to be so direct, but you asked me to be clear."

The man's throat immediately went dry. "Dying?"

"It will be gradual." The doctor gave a little cough.

"What are the prospects for a man without dopamine?"

"Rather dreary, if I may say so. Dopamine plays a role in sensations, feelings of pleasure and desire, among other things."

Another silence.

"Are you following me?"

"I was asking myself whether I had, over the past two or three weeks, felt pleasure or desire."

"What I'm saying shouldn't be taken too literally. Anyway, dopamine is also responsible for coordination, and that's where things really get serious. The trembling in your right hand is slight but very characteristic."

The man closed his eyes and an image appeared: his mother trying to bring a glass to her mouth, then giving up. He remembers the movement she made, the slight sound of the glass being set down on the table. And then another memory: his mother stuck, like him, with independent hands, the left hand holding down the right one, the crazy hand that had to be stilled and hidden.

"It can be treated quite effectively today. With appropriate medication, you can hope ..."

"... to live many years in relatively good health, especially if you have family and friends to cheer you up and spoon-feed you."

"Don't take it so badly."

"How would *you* take it?"

"There's a new method being tested. Electrodes implanted in the spinal cord. It should allow Parkinson's patients to walk more normally."

"But I walk normally."

"Hmm ... not really."

"And my deflated sacs? My engorged alveoli? What do you do with them with Parkinson's in the picture?"

The doctor scribbled something about something.

"Am I going to die of suffocation?" the man insisted. "Am I going to tremble until the end of my days and then die of suffocation?"

"You're suffering from anxiety, sir."

"I don't want to die of suffocation. Anything but that."

"Anxiety is a normal phenomenon, especially for a person who's solitary."

"How do you know that?"

"If you only knew how many poor wretches end up in the hospital on Saturday night!"

"It's Wednesday today."

"If you only knew how many poor wretches end up in the hospital on Wednesday night!"

"How long?"

The doctor raised his head, indicating the clock – a big round thing flat as a pancake – which led the man to think he had only a few hours to live, a few minutes, even. His breathing quickened.

"Is that all?"

The doctor gave him a prescription and left him there, advising him to enjoy himself a little.

35

When he got home, he collapsed. Two whole days, during which he did nothing but breathe, drink, eat, evacuate, all with an exemplary economy of action and movement.

Later, he collapsed a second time, outside in the snow, to be exact, in front of the window of a convenience store on which was written in glowing yellow letters: Open 24 Hours a Day, Even at Night.

The convenience store clerk did what he did twenty-four hours a day: he was convenient. Abandoning the long line of customers waiting to buy their lottery tickets, he hurried out to help Number 32 lying in front of his door. Realizing he would never be able to do anything alone, he went back inside in just as much of a hurry to ask the aspiring Fresh Starters for help. It took some convincing, and finally, actual pushing, to get them outside to lift the mastodon, transport him inside, and put him down on the floor between the durum-wheat pasta and the cholesterol-free potato chips.

Number 32 regained consciousness a few minutes later and categorically refused to let them call an ambulance. The convenience store clerk immediately deduced, with the astounding lucidity of the simple-minded, that the man was drunk or was not right in the head, two states that more or less summed up the human condition, at least those representatives of it that he encountered on a daily basis.

5

I am the end in itself.

I work in the already no more, the consumed, the so quickly finished. Healing a sick person, building an airplane, pushing out a fetus all have a future; they open, they lead to something, and if I may say so, there is necessarily an after. Whereas with me, it's about yesterday.

But life leaves marks, traces. Like the old gent brought to me with his hand still clutching his penis, and what a job it was detaching it to return it to a more noble position. Like another one with his mouth open so wide that his tonsils were as dry and black as overcooked liver. What is that if it isn't life? It's pleasure after the fact, delayed fear, marks, traces. The soul that sniffs the body and fears for its life, the worst cases for me.

I work with the traces.

They've just brought me a child. A boy. Six or seven years old. Hit by a car. The left leg is completely swollen, but the body is intact, still suntanned in spite of the winter. There's a darker line at the waist where the sun got in above the bathing suit, which miraculously preserved the whiteness of the skin. The boy looks like he's sleeping, his face turned toward me. Once I would have gone away and left everything there. I would have waited two days. For what? For him to wake up, stretch like a kitten, yawn, smile, reach out his arms and say, "I'm hungry." His parents would have protested. Black mark on my record. "Care for the dead," my father had said. Saving the bodies is also caring for them.

Twice in a row I failed the exam to become a doctor. After my second failure, my father looked up from his newspaper one morning and said, "If you can't take care of the living, take care of the dead."

I looked up in turn, intrigued by the calm with which he had greeted the news of my failure.

"Why not?" he continued. "Care for the dead."

The dead.

The idea seemed ridiculous to me at first, but little by little it took hold, until it became as tenacious as the smell of formalin that, twenty-one years later, follows me everywhere. My father died shortly after our brief conversation, probably so that he wouldn't have to breathe the smell, which would have reminded him of what he must have considered a loss of status.

So I became an embalmer. Or a mortician, if you prefer, but I detest the word, which is as cold and aseptic as a surgical instrument. "The Egyptians embalmed," a colleague once said, correcting me on my use of the word. "We are morticians. There's a difference."

I wash the boy from head to toe. The procedure takes time, and I work gently so that he doesn't suffer, barely touching his leg. The boy is very small in the middle of the table. His downy blond hair stands up and shines.

Then, I read. Out of respect, but also for the sounds. There's nothing more musical than a corpse ... rigidity setting in, putrefaction suddenly relaxing a limb or a muscle, liquids oozing out. As if once the floodgates are opened, the body forgets all modesty and wants only to spread out, to let go of life, the way rats desert a sinking ship.

And then I stand up, time and time again. I carry out movements, always the same ones. Same movements, same objects, the utensils of death. Injection, aspiration, fluids for fluids, formalin for blood, conservation for life. I can't help it, each time I press down on the syringe, I have the impression I'm causing death. It has been a long time since we eviscerated the corpses. Today, we do things quickly and efficiently, we pump the arteries full of solutions so powerful that I'm always surprised the poor devil doesn't sit up and punch me in the face. And the siphon that aspirates, all the blood spilled, so much, it's unimaginable, the blood drains, then the formalin, after that it will be over and it will be too late, I mean, life will be well and truly driven out. The body too. The fire, the heat, a thousand degrees, it's a lot. The dust that will fill the air in the lab for hours, to the point of chasing me outside and making me run like a madman.

I think a great deal. But contrary to what one might imagine, especially since Descartes, I *am* no more than anyone else. I *am* normally. But I think. The most innocuous corpse lands on my table and *wham!* its whole history pops up, with a beginning, a middle, and an end. I only have the end, and I imagine a middle and a beginning. It's the beginning that hurts. Then I go out, I run, I survey the land, the thing that is the surest. I look at the trees, trees, and more trees, everything that stands up. The trunks rising up from the ground, the masses of branches thrusting into the sky. We reach up, it's inevitable.

"Don't you find your work depressing?"

"Oh, I'm an optimist by nature! I tell myself that one day I'll come across a live one. It's just a matter of probabilities."

6

"All this for you?"

Number 32 nods his head. The pharmacist shakes his as he reads the endless list of medications prescribed.

"Well, what do you know!"

Then he notices the date. Instead of asking, "Why did you wait so long?" which would be normal, he asks, "Why now?"

Why *now*, indeed? What could make a developing Parkinsonian, a genuine sick person, decide to come out of his hibernation and embark on the great adventure of life?

"It's spring," Number 32 simply says.

The answer wends its tortuous way through the pharmacist's neurons, but gets lost en route. An arsenal of drugs has appeared on the counter. The rattle of pills on the plastic tray. Counting. "If you continue at this rate," the doctor had said. At what rate, for goodness' sake? Is playing the piano twenty-two hours a day not a normal rate for a pianist? Maybe not, no. Not for thirty-five years straight. Why couldn't a person devote himself to a single thing? Why should you have to be versatile? Because there's everything else. What else? The rest of life, surely. But what life?

Life.

People come in and go out, on their way to work, on their way home. A labourer in blue work clothes puts a chocolate bar on the counter, searches in his pockets, and throws a bill down without waiting for change. Number 32 heads for the door, his pockets stuffed with bottles of various sizes filled with pills of various colours. "The yellow ones are to be taken on an empty stomach, the white ones after lunch, and the black ones at night." The black ones at night.

As he goes through the door, images from another age pop into his head: a cold morning in spring, his chubby hands opening, spreading out, his white fingers on the big Schimmel, the ivory teeth you press to bring forth sounds, and his father, his father getting up and shutting himself in his museum, the final sound of the key, the house stuffed with costly little things …

He suddenly feels ill. No chair in sight, and in any case just one would not have been enough. The pharmacist looks up just then and comes over to him.

"Are you okay?"

He nods, yes, yes, and straightens up. A long sinuous, animal movement.

"The least expensive?"

Usually I'm the one who suggests the coffin. I look at the client's face, clothes, general appearance, and I suggest oak, maple, or cherry. Dying is expensive, wood is a luxury commodity, but still, you can't bury the dead in cardboard boxes.

"What I'm asking you is simple," he says. "I want the least expensive coffin."

Usually, also, I'm the one who talks, not the client. The helping relationship is the mortician's business. *Sympathize without overdoing it, be courteous, discreet, politely sad. Practise empathy.* We've learned how to act.

"I thought you would like …"

"Don't worry about what I'd like, worry about what I tell you. I don't intend to spend a penny on her."

The *her* in question is a tall woman of about fifty with soft features and a body that's still beautiful. Another principle that must never be forgotten: *the attachment of the bereaved to the remains*.

"But don't you think she …"

"Not a penny, I said."

Empathy. See the subject coming, raise it yourself first. Gently. They don't talk and don't want anything, they are overcome and don't have the least idea of what's good for them. Communication in its pure state is the mortician's greatest asset, his superiority. I take a breath.

"Contrary to what you may think, our role is not limited to communing with organs, which can be a bit repetitive. We also provide support to the bereaved."

He raises a haughty eyebrow. "Support whatever you want, my good man, I don't care one bit."

Sympathize and anticipate. When possible, of course.

"In that case, I suggest …"

"Dispose of the body, that's all I'm asking you to do."

"Understood. I'll cut it in pieces and throw it in the garbage. Two green bags, the cheapest ones. Is that what you want?"

He stands up and places two flushed paws on the desk. He's going to shout. I stand up in turn.

"Get out of here! I'll take care of her."

I won't have anyone telling me what to do with my dead people. I'm very touchy about that.

7

"I'd like to entrust this to you," says Hu, handing me a big brown envelope.

He gives me a devastating wink and immediately lowers his eyes like a repentant child.

I know that look. That provocative humility, look what I've done. The big soft package reeks of autobiography. I read a lot and it shows, so they take advantage and give me their written lives for assessment. Since they don't have much ahead of them anymore, they look behind them and put it down in writing. They want to know if it was worth the trouble, all that trouble, getting up in the morning, behaving, living 365 days a year for 110 years. I have three piles of lives on my night table. Three piles of four lives each, for a total of twelve. Not yet read.

Hu's two black slits are peering at me, they haven't faded, time has preserved their colour. Nothing like Mrs. Le Chevalier's or Mrs. de Valois's transparent pupils. "I'd like to entrust this to you," Hu says. Yet it's not a parrot or a hamster. They are entrusting their lives to me, and they will entrust their deaths to me. Could it be that, without knowing it, I am a whole person?

And then I relent, I give in. I always give in. I take the envelope, my arm bends, thirteen lives to read and assess.

Their faces become a little more wrinkled and they go on their way. Backs bent, quick little steps, relieved, that's done.

∾

Fortunately, bad luck never comes alone, good luck always comes along with it. Mrs. de Valois — another tenant, one of those I didn't mention out of tact and respect for confidentiality — is leaving the building accompanied by her cane, her canvas, and her easel. She too is wooing me, though I haven't given any sign of painting. "It's because you're young," she says. "I want to know what a young person today understands about modern painting."

Since I can't relieve her of her cane, I hoist the big pale frame up onto my right shoulder and slip the canvas under one or the other of my arms, and off we go. This is always a great moment, because people look at me completely differently; that is, they look at me. Arm in arm, we proceed to the park, she with a lightened load and I heavy of art and soul. I converse, I traverse streets and avenues, she on my right, I on her left, I smile at passersby who imagine that Mrs. de Valois is my model and I'm a painter who works in restoration. Going past the fruit stalls, I compress and gather myself; I have to or the long legs of the easel could knock things down. I do it with the ease that befits a painter; you can see right away that I'm used to it. When we arrive at the park, I unload, and the easel stands on its own. Mrs. de Valois sits down on a bench, always the same one. We have our habits. She thanks me, I thank her; she doesn't understand why, I do. From the building to the park, I is another, which is very gratifying.

The only trouble is that Mrs. de Valois's sketch is not at all lifelike. I'm just saying that, of course, I'm not a painter, but people shouldn't think you don't know anything just because you embalm. I also draw, I remodel faces, I have to, if you could see the condition they come to us in, sometimes they don't even have their heads anymore. We're all sculptors at heart but we never talk about it, prejudices are persistent.

Anyway, in my opinion, Mrs. de Valois doesn't see well. At her age, that's to be expected, but it hurts to see the painting. Oh my, the painting is really off the mark! That big circle there in the middle is the pond, those grey blotches are the water spraying from the fountain, and that scratch, a passerby, I'd swear to it. But talk about a pond, talk about a passerby, kind of a flame veering forward as if in a hurry to get it over with. Passersby are elusive creatures, they never stay in one place very long, try to pin them down and they've passed by, it's an impasse. But as sure as my name is Hermann, she'll never make me believe there's a skeleton there; it's soft, without any anatomy to speak of.

I summon up my courage. "That is incompatible with the pelvic bone, Mrs. de Valois. Not to mention the spine."

She looks up at me with her beautiful colourless eyes. "What are you talking about, my boy?"

"The spinal column. Your walkers there, they're … nothing at all, that thing there …"

"What thing?"

"That swaying mass, nobody walks like that … And this round thing here, this circle …"

Mrs. de Valois waits, her brush raised. "Keep going, my boy, express yourself."

"Talk about a pond! There are limits to the lack of verisimilitude."

"But where do you see a pond?"

I point to the pond in the park, the real one, with the fountain in the middle. "It flows, it gushes, it forms drops, while yours …"

Mrs. de Valois looks at the pond and the fountain without showing the least sign of recognition.

"We come here every day, Mrs. de Valois, and every day you paint, well, you try to paint, this pond and this fountain. I understand that you can be sidetracked by unstable walkers, but the pond and the fountain, those don't change."

"But look, my boy, just because we come to the park every day doesn't mean I should feel obligated to paint it."

"What's the point of coming here, then?"

I leave her to herself, certain that she prefers to be alone to make a career change to something recognizable. It's a rough time for her, like me when I changed from life to death.

I head to the lab, unburdened of art but with a weight on my soul, that of Hu. I pass the stalls again and I stop. The manuscript is heavy and I put it down. There's fruit there, not very abundant, without much colour, the forced premature fruit of spring.

8

The fruit is colourless and insipid, thinks Number 32. He walks around the merchant's stall and feels the plums, the peaches, the limes, one after the other. Furtively. Not so much because he doesn't want to be seen fingering them – some merchants loathe the practice – but because it requires his hands and he doesn't want anyone to see them trembling. Since he was labelled as having Parkinson's, he's been showing extra concern for them.

The peaches are green and hard as rocks. There's a big brown envelope lying next to them. He picks it up and examines it. Two names side by side – Hermann and Hu – as if the addressee and the sender were interchangeable, and a single address, hastily scribbled: 72 des Échelles Street.

He goes to the cash and puts down a dozen lemons, six oranges, a bag of onions, and the big brown envelope.

"Somebody forgot this," he says.

The merchant shrugs, takes the envelope, and drops it unceremoniously on the ground next to the garbage cans, anywhere but on his fruit.

Number 32 pays and walks away, then turns back, picks up the envelope, and sticks it under his left arm. He goes home by way of the park and sits down not far from the old lady to watch her paint. He has a bit of trouble with old people, he usually doesn't see them, so much decrepitude, it's not possible, we can't become *that*, but there's something soothing about this old woman. The man thinks to himself that it's because she's doing something. She's painting a circle, always the same one, with two glowing black spots in the middle.

At a certain point, she feels his gaze on her and turns her head toward him.

"What are you looking at, young man?"

"Your hands. I'm looking at your hands."

"What about my hands?"

"They're delicate, graceful …"

She looks down at his hands – two flat oysters resting on his fat knees. He hasn't had time to hide them and the twisted index finger is very visible.

"I can't say the same for yours, my friend."

"No, you can't."

"What kind of work do you do?"

He makes the evasive gesture of a person who doesn't want to talk about himself.

"Hands like yours are surely very useful for doing certain things."

"Yes, but what things?"

He smiles, he's so big, he looks so placid, as if he's seen it all, that of course she's not at all wary of him.

"Heavy work, for example. Driving tractors, moving furniture. A big strapping fellow like you. Hands like that are useful. Are you a longshoreman? A mover?"

Driving tractors, moving furniture. It's so naive, so simple and innocent, that he suddenly bursts out laughing. The old lady gives a start, tottering on her fragile base. He'd like to say, "I'm a pianist. At least I was until very recently. Now I don't know anymore."

She's gone back to her work, her forehead marked with a fine crease. She's painting from memory, without a model, her impatient brush going over and over the circle with its two little disks in the middle.

"Do you think you can rely on appearances, madam?"

"What do you mean?"

"I don't drive tractors." "I never claimed you did."

"But you think my physical appearance suggests it."

"Goodness, yes. Just like me," she adds, for fear of having hurt him. "Who would think, looking at me, that I have a passion for painting?"

"Everyone."

"Thank you, my boy," she says after a moment's hesitation.

She makes as if to go back to her painting, but turns to him again.

"I didn't mean to offend you."

"No offence, madam." (He smiles again.) "I do indeed drive tractors. You got it right."

She looks at him, relieved. "I don't think you can rely on appearances, but I also don't think that the outer envelope is completely without meaning."

～

He walks with no precise destination, pacing the streets with his fruit and the big envelope under his arm. He goes past the park three times, past the drugstore four times. He has never wandered around this way, rudderless and aimless. Agents, secretaries, impresarios. They always had a program to wave around, a concert, a tour, such full schedules. He has never had to manage his time; in fact, he has never had to fill his time. But when you have air sacs that refuse to inflate and anarchic hands that move without your asking them to, you're permitted to wander a little, to look weird and to think intently about the future. He's not rich and has never been poor, that's not the question. The question is: what future? What to do now? He walks looking at his feet and his strong knees that barely stick out under the fabric. From time to time, he nods, as if the sidewalk has given him an answer. He has put on his cape – a long black cloak with little sleeves in which anyone but him would look ridiculous but which gives him a certain style. He walks quickly, the cloak swirling around his legs. Something has given way, the old life is crumbling, falling apart.

Useful. His lips pronounce the word silently several times in a row, savouring it with a tiny hesitation, as if tasting a dish for the first time. Useful and versatile. Exactly what does that mean? His footsteps lead him quite naturally to the port. It's the route he likes the best, because the street slopes down gently as if it too were drawn to the sea. It's not the sea, it's just water, viscous, dirty water that, at night, when the moon is shining, can give the illusion of being clean. The little port is teeming with life, and that's also what he comes there looking for, life, cafés, movie theatres. The same bum is there too, faithful as always, wobbly but still standing, who greets him each time by bowing to the ground in an obsequious gesture that may express either deference or sarcasm.

He heads back up, goes into the café, orders a beer, and sits down at a table in the back, the one that gives him a view of the water and Yseult. Sometimes she's there, sometimes not. She must be around thirty-five and doesn't talk much, but when she's there, he feels like just anybody, an ordinary man moved by the presence of a woman. She has long, very straight black hair, with bangs that partly hide her eyes and that she pushes back when she leans over to take the orders. He doesn't know if he finds her attractive, all he knows is that when she's close, there's a kind of vibration in the air that catches him off guard. She may know nothing about music, rheumatoid arthritis, or fading talent, but she gets the atoms excited, she really does.

Sometimes he imagines going upstairs with her. That's the end of the spectacle of the water, but there's the bedroom. The walls are blue, with reproductions pasted up, an observation that causes him a feeling of dismay, almost pity. You can't change the way you are, not when you have a father who's obsessed with Byzantine miniatures. Here Renoir, Bonnard, Millet gleam under their plastic film. Standing in the bedroom, he looks at them without batting an eye, trying not to let them get to him. "It's because of the humidity," Yseult says. "This way, they don't warp as much." He turns around and looks at her, and she has that funny, confused smile she always gives him when she has to throw him out because the café is closing. It wouldn't bother him if they did it amid the laminated classics of art. He's no expert on things sexual, but he thinks it would be okay. He only wonders what Renoir, Bonnard, and Millet would think, if they would feel confined in their synthetic envelopes and if they wouldn't prefer living in the open air, even if they warped, even if their colours slowly faded, going from bright to dull, from dull to almost nothing. To nothing.

Yseult has a voice that sets him vibrating. It's not rare that at the height of their transports he'll ask her to talk, not to whisper, he would hate that, but to talk, to speak words, any words, out loud. Yseult can't bring herself to do it, she's too shy, so he gives her books and poems. She's the one who chooses. So as not to have to get up in the heat of the action, she learns entire texts by heart, and when the time comes, recites them in her beautiful husky, studied voice. Under the warm caress, he curls up and pulls in his neck. The image that comes to him then is one of a bird regurgitating food into the beak of its young. The young bird is him. That changes him, for once.

9

In the evening, I go home by way of the park — I always go through the park to bring back Mrs. de Valois's easel and canvas. It's another one of my great moments, the painter weary but happy with a job well done. The only thing I'm afraid of is that someone will stop me and ask what on earth I'm trying to reproduce. If that ever happens, I risk being torn between my affection for Mrs. de Valois and my reputation as a painter. After all, I have my pride. All those crude shapes, the two scratches with the circle of the fake pond and the spray of water that refuses to be wet ... I don't want at any price ever to have to answer for that, neither for that nor for the title: *Wanderings*. So I amble along with the canvas turned over, with Mrs. de Valois's pathetic efforts against my abdomen. Face is saved, my own and Mrs. de Valois's.

～

And then, catastrophe: on my way home, I see Hu.

After a moment of uncertainty, the memory comes back to me ... oh my God! The manuscript, the canvas, the easel, the anemic peaches, the manuscript left there.

I rush to the fruit seller's, which has already closed. I throw myself at the door and bang on it. Let me in, for God's sake! I've lost a life, do you hear me? An original life, for sure, those old people have long ago given up reproduction in all its forms.

Going into my building for the second time, I meet Mrs. Le Chevalier coming out.

"Hello, Mrs. Le Chevalier."

She stops, surprised. "Is that all?"

I stop, surprised.

"And your usual words? Your ten elastic years?"

"No, not tonight."

~

The next day, first thing in the morning, at the fruit seller's.

"I forgot a manuscript here yesterday. There, beside the peaches, to be precise."

A manuscript. He looks at me, incredulous. The word is not edible, it hasn't a single vitamin, and besides … In short, the fruit seller doesn't understand.

"A pile of paper this high," I say, forming a *C* with my hand. "In a brown envelope."

"Oh, that!"

He hesitates, he's vague, everything's vague.

"There, I guess," he says, pointing his index finger.

There. All I see is a big groaning grey metal backside, flanked by two workers who are lifting bins and garbage cans and emptying them into it.

No, not that! It can't be. I refuse to accept it. There must be a god of lost manuscripts. And there isn't a single Boisvert-Dufradel in sight. The ones who are always poking around everywhere, untying knots and pulling out marvellous things. How can it be that not one of them was on the lookout?

I run all the way home, arrive ahead of the big backside, climb the stairs, and hammer on the Boisvert-Dufradels' door; they're usually out and about early with the garbage cans. Mrs. Boisvert-Dufradel comes to the door with her usual inquisitive look.

"I … I've lost some papers. They're down there, in the backside … I mean, in the belly of the beast."

She doesn't get it, acts slow. In the morning light, she looks a lot less determined, she has that vague expression that precedes makeup, and her dressing gown is non-standard.

"So what is it to me?" she asks curtly.

You can't have it all, recycling and being pleasant. And

then, this is the first time I've asked her for anything. Being avoided year in, year out by a building full of golden agers can make a person sour.

"Please help me. I need you."

Mrs. Boisvert-Dufradel hesitates between my permanent total lack of interest in her and my sudden attentiveness. Out back, or I should say down below, the noise grows louder.

"It's here," I say. "Come, you're the only one who can convince them to give me back my papers."

Without a word, she follows me, agrees to deal with the situation. Once outside, she positions herself right in the middle of the street.

"Stop!" she cries, raising a forceful hand in front of the garbage truck.

The two men act as if they haven't seen or heard anything, bustling about even more. They obviously know her. I should have thought of that. They're old adversaries, you can sense it. If Mrs. Boisvert-Dufradel goes after the least little individual garbage can, just think what she'll do with a collective trash receptacle.

Mrs. Boisvert-Dufradel, however, is unfazed. She puts her fists on her hips and waits. The two men hang from the truck like bunches of grapes and the driver puts it in gear again. Mrs. Boisvert-Dufradel stands firm. It's like in a movie, there's the big machine advancing and that frail, fragile little thing in her old-fashioned dressing gown. The machine keeps moving forward until it's touching her dressing gown, but she doesn't budge, the huge beast insists, she resists, it's great cinema. The truck goes *vroom! vroom!* and then gives up and stops. A foul-smelling sigh. Mrs. Boisvert-Dufradel hasn't flinched.

She looks at me and gives me one of her big white smiles. It's crazy, but I was starting to feel strangely lonesome for her teeth. She gestures toward the truck with her chin. "Go ahead, help yourself, don't stand on ceremony."

I walk around the backside. "I'm looking for some papers ..."

One of the bunches of grapes drops to the ground. "Papers? Is that all!"

He pulls a lever, opens a huge maw (not his own, of course) and reveals a nauseating grey paste that's begging to go back into the ground.

"It was brown," I add because I don't know what else to say and because that conglomeration is depressing.

"Brown ..." sighs the worker.

Suddenly, I spot something in the vile mess, an object sticking out, a tiny black ring pointing upward, refusing to blend in. I slip a finger into the ring and yank it as if I were fishing out a drowned body. The ring comes out by itself, without its load of autobiography. No problem! I plunge both hands into the grey mass and pull out all sorts of things more or less unworthy of mention. Mrs. Boisvert-Dufradel comes over, filled with envy. The two men swoop down on her.

"If you touch a single hair ..."

And it's true that there's hair, lots of it, the weekly oily waste from the beauty parlour across the street, absurdly mixed with carrot and potato peels, dirty kitty litter, and so on. A life buried in slime. Because I have the manuscript, I'm holding it in my stinking hands, two hundred sticky sheets that have fallen out of the open envelope.

I carry it home under the approving gaze of Mrs. Boisvert-Dufradel. I put the whole thing down on the kitchen counter and clean it as best I can. My cats jump onto the counter, which they never do because they've been well brought up, but this is too much for them, it's like a siren call, the old forgotten smells of street garbage.

～

My two last hopes were that Hu would immediately die or that he'd forget the events of his own life – but not everyone is lucky enough to get amnesia.

The document was illegible. In the rare places that were

free of stains, I could make out diagrams, perhaps drawings, and numbers, endless columns of numbers. Hu was not an accountant. He had neither the appearance nor the assurance, nor, I'd have wagered, the rigour. An accountant does not entrust his financial statements to a mortician.

I collapsed. What I was looking at must be an old annual report. I really and truly had lost Hu's manuscript.

There were two possible solutions available to me: to avoid Hu like the plague until the end of his days or to rewrite his life.

I opted for the safest solution: to rewrite Hu's life *and* to avoid him like the plague.

10

Useful. He can't shake the word. Unless it's the idea. A pianist is not someone useful – or at least, only in the figurative sense. Useful for inner life, for access to intangible worlds. But useful in the sense of necessary, no, certainly not. A useful person provides a service, satisfies a need, but I don't, Number 32 says to himself. He wanders along the docks among the carefree, idle strollers, hoping to pass unnoticed. That's reckoning without his corpulence or the spring night that, after a radiant May day, is refusing to fall. And that's reckoning without the fact that he's neither carefree nor idle. He's immediately noticeable, a giant dressed in black silk, his neck stretched painfully toward the dilapidated walls wet with filth, eyes alert looking for what? The unthinkable, no less. A future more in keeping with his appearance, a way to break through the blind walls that have been put up in front of him.

And he does indeed notice something, a dirty white rectangle attached with thumbtacks to the door of a storage shed. The fourth thumbtack has fallen out and the paper is flapping in the breeze. He goes over and presses his nose to the door – night is starting to fall after all, and he can't see well. "We're hiring," says the little piece of paper. And lower down:

> *Roving Heavy-Duty Dockworker Wanted*
> *Please apply to the office.*
> *Open from 6 a.m. to noon and from 1 p.m. to 4 p.m., not a second longer.*

He remains standing in front of the ad, reading and rereading it several times. Intrigued by so much attention being paid to such a short text, the strollers stop for a moment and come over, perhaps hoping for a revelation or the solution to an insoluble problem. Disappointed, they walk away grumbling. Some turn back to examine the big man whose eyes still haven't left the little ad. Must be half blind, they think, or maybe illiterate.

～

He looks at himself in the big full-length mirror that stands in one corner of the bedroom and wonders if he could possibly be that roving heavy-duty dockworker. Heavy, yes, without a doubt. A dockworker, maybe. Roving? Why not? I'm already that. Travelling around the world, going from city to city giving concerts, I've done that my whole life. I *am* a roving heavy pianist.

> *Longshoreman (noun): person who loads and unloads ships using machines and equipment (cranes, mechanical winches, etc.). A longshoreman must have a certain amount of physical strength. The tasks entrusted to him require attention to detail and vigilance, so that people are not put in danger and equipment and merchandise are not damaged.*

I can do that, Number 32 concludes. I don't see why a pianist who has spent most of his life interpreting difficult works wouldn't be able to move packages. For a moment, courage returns, hope is revived. No, sir, life doesn't stop here. Beside the dictionary on the bookshelf, a book on career options is slowly disintegrating under its dried-up cover. His father acquired it shortly after his birth to try to predict the prospects for a child who clearly had little affinity for miniatures and who, despite repeated warnings, would get hold of his precious figurines without taking the customary precautions; that is, washing his hands, sitting down with a responsible adult, and remaining motionless until the responsible adult has stored the little objects in their purple velvet cases. The chapter on the RIASEC typology, also known as the Holland Codes, had been consulted more than the others, the dog-eared pages confirmed the father's interest in this typology, which classified six types of human beings with respect to career choice: Realistic, Investigative, Artistic, Social, Enterprising, and Conventional.

He reads through each of the descriptions and immediately dismisses all the types except Artistic, but not without first wondering what conclusions his father had reached. He's struck by the words *sensitive*, *creative*, *intuitive*, *passionate*, *imaginative*. Artistic types express themselves freely, based on their perceptions, sensibility, and intuition. They are original, nonconformist, and at ease in situations that are out of the ordinary. Number 32 raises his head, stunned. He has never seen himself this way, he has never seen so clearly laid out what has until now been his pride. His throat tightens, he has a feeling of having missed out, not on happiness, but on himself, on that great, happy, fulfilled person he was without knowing it.

And what am I now? he wonders. Can you change category from one day to the next? Does the category you belong to abandon you, or does it leave marks, deep, indelible traces? And if I'm no longer the Artistic type, who am I? Certainly not Investigative. I'm not particularly observant, I don't like playing with ideas, I'm not logical or objective, and I hate solving problems. Social? Even less. I'm kind of a bear – bear Number 32 – who since childhood has been lugging around a tired piano that nobody cares about anymore. The Enterprising and Conventional types are even further from the image he has of himself.

That leaves the Realistic type. Aren't all people, at some point or other in their lives, realistic? If only to find their way around, feed themselves, and keep their houses clean. Realistic people are good with their hands and at ease with practical tasks, tools, and heavy machinery. Number 32 has a tender thought for the painter with the tractors and wonders if he himself is as patient, meticulous, stable, and sensible as the RIASEC occupational typology describes. Fortunately, the book notes that every occupation is a combination of several types. I am thus the Artistic-Realistic type with a touch of Enterprising.

He goes back to the port, making a wide detour through the park. The painter isn't there. In her place, there's a small crowd gathered around a body lying on the ground. Usually he avoids such spectacles, but curiosity gets the better of him and he goes over. In the midst of the leaning onlookers, there's a man of about fifty who looks like he's asleep. A bicycle is lying next to him, intact, and the front wheel is still turning with a soft metallic hiss. The cyclist's face is serene, relaxed. His two arms extend outward from his body as if he had agreed to stretch out and let the earth permeate him, and one of his legs is bent, the foot flat on the ground. His eyes are closed; his lips, full, red, and moist; a wisp of grey hair lies across his forehead. Why him and not me? wonders Number 32. If his heart has stopped, why couldn't mine? Not unless I spent twenty-two hours a day cycling. Artistic-Realistic-Enterprising-Athletic?

He hangs around the port. He has read the ad again and again, and now he's walking back and forth in front of the office. He encourages himself with Artistic-Realistic-Enterprising. Through the glass door, a woman who has her back to him is busy at a worn Formica counter of indeterminate colour. A man is doing something beside her with a lot of fuss.

He goes over, his hand extended to give three little knocks and grab the doorknob. At the last minute, he changes his mind, backs up a few steps, takes in with a single one of his anxious glances the not very tall but oh so menacing building. Then he walks away, strides along the docks, comes back, constantly doubting himself, hesitating. Artistic-Realistic-Enterprising. The atmosphere of the port gradually permeates him, its hum, its smells, its feverish activity punctuated with men's shouts — he's never felt the brute force of the presence of men at work as he does here — he stops and watches them, starts to attract notice, to be in the way, perhaps. There's nothing worse than an old man who's starting over.

And then everything stops. The well-oiled machine that

was so recently purring, surrounded with skilled care, all those mobile men executing serious, difficult movements with an assurance that touched him deeply – Realistic, Enterprising, and Conventional types, without doubt – suddenly it all stops. In an instant, the docks empty and the boats that were so animated, so filled with people, look like deserted ruins. He thinks of a theatre abandoned by its actors without a goodbye, of the hurrying spectators already outside, clumsily putting their coats on, lighting cigarettes, hailing taxis. Such abruptness shocks him. He never abandoned his piano that way. And he was the one who decided when it was over, not the clock. He would stand up quietly, knowing he would not get anything more out of the instrument but remaining there for a few moments, a little to the side, while the sounds died out by themselves. Anthropomorphic Artistic, the worst case, which is not found in any book.

He goes home exhausted, more perplexed than ever.

"Do you want me to choose for you?"

The woman shakes her head and leafs through the catalogue for the third time, using the tips of her fingers, looking disgusted. She's at least sixty-three years old, but she has made every effort to appear forty-seven. The eyes faded a long time ago and the pinched mouth closed on a complaint forever stifled. Her dead person is beside her, brought in this morning, a solid, smooth man.

She continues leafing absent-mindedly through the catalogue. She's not looking at me, and she won't for anything in the world.

"I asked you a question, madam."

This time she raises her head and her torso pulls back almost imperceptibly, as if she could conceivably envisage looking at me from a distance. I've obviously offended her. One mustn't pressure people under such circumstances.

"Why don't you leave it to me? The choice of the coffin is clearly of no interest to you. That's not a criticism, I assure you. Nobody is interested in this kind of thing. Except me, of course, and even then."

I would have liked to see her smile, just out of curiosity, to see if a contraction was possible without disrupting the overall organization of her facial muscles.

"Besides, we're wasting our time, the coffin is already ordered. Someone came this morning."

Another woman, younger, not as pretty but so much sadder. Rushing in breathless and embarrassed, to be the first, at least one time. It's always the same story.

The woman leaps to her feet, walks to the window, inhales with convulsive movements of her offended shoulders.

"I'm not telling you anything you don't know, madam. I'm just trying to say that the coffin has already been chosen. And paid for. Two coffins for one body seems excessive to me. I didn't know how to tell you. It's done."

She paces back and forth in the office, wringing her hands. She has bearing, elegance, no more smooth husband, and the confirmation that he was enjoying himself with another woman. Her clothes are luxurious, they cling to her body and fall nicely.

She takes forever to leave.

11

I feel Zita's breath on my neck, I see her attentive profile. I sometimes have these falls, these absurdly painful air pockets that are called doubts and that temporarily deprive me of oxygen. Zita in her multipocket jumpsuit, Zita eminently supple, with her muscles that must snap back into place by themselves when they're moved. I don't know, I've never moved them.

Zita has two shoulders, a neck, black eyes and hair, long muscles, very alive tissues, and fabulous popliteal hollows. In addition, she is anergic, which is very practical in the profession. Unlike many of our interns, whose skin turns red at the mere sight of the chemicals lined up on our counters — it's true there are a lot of them, all proudly displaying their skull and crossbones — Zita's organism valiantly resists corrosion and does not seem at all discommoded by the fetid emanations that permeate the air in our laboratories.

The trouble is that I don't know where or when I'll see her again. Her internship ended months ago, and I didn't say anything. As for her, she hasn't gotten in touch. But what if she showed up one day? What if, one fine morning, I found her on my doorstep, with her big smile and her husky voice saying, "Here I am, I've been waiting so long for you"? I firmly believe in things that cannot be. Meanwhile, I'm at the ready, always presentable, freshly shaven in case she wouldn't like my beard, clean and properly dressed. It's a bit tiresome, because everyone has a right to completely let go, to be at home and look like a slob if they feel like it, that's what houses are made for. My elderly lady friends are constantly complimenting me on my appearance: "You take such good care of yourself, Mr. Hermann! Such elegance! That grey coat puts colour in your face, you're always so pale!"

Sometimes I tell myself that's not the way to meet people, that I should give luck a boost and at least telephone Zita. I can't. Do you ask an antelope to pounce on a hunter? No, a hundred times no. I'm no hunter, I'm the solitary antelope type that pounces on nothing and no one. So I do as the antelopes of the world do: I wait.

～

"There's way too much."

"No, there isn't," says Julian.

The judge is abnormally ruddy. He came to us pallid and defeated, and now he's bursting with health. The resources of the mortician's trade are surprising. Formalin bleaches the tissues, so we use makeup to correct the "inappropriate discoloration." And we have our code of honour: bodies should not be sullied by anything macabre. But Julian always puts on too much, his bodies are always too pink. Julian suffers from a free hand and an exaggerated code of honour.

"I'm telling you there is. Think of the family, Julian. They won't recognize him like that."

Julian shrugs and extracts one of his surprising brown candies from his pocket. If I didn't have absolute confidence in him, I'd swear it was a dog biscuit. Fortunately, he never swallows them. We have to be cautious here with everything that tries to get at us through our mouths.

I go over to the table, grab a rag, and wipe the cheeks, which is never done once the artist has signed his work.

"A judge that red isn't normal," Alfred declares as he walks in.

"Tell that to Julian."

"It's a case of 'inappropriate coloration'," says Alfred, trying to be funny.

Alfred and Julian have been partners for ten years. Since they decided together to get out of the company where a monster by the name of Burgess, a sad person with a threatening gaze, seemed to take an idiotic pleasure in maintaining a reign of terror. He established his authority by setting up his office by the entrance and watching people's comings and goings, keeping tabs on their arrival and departure times, unfortunately for Alfred, who was always late.

One day, they had reported to work to find Burgess looking delighted and displaying a brand new time clock like a hard-won trophy.

Julian was the first to protest, Julian the silent one who only opens his mouth to say yes, no, how are you? He told Burgess that there was absolutely no question of his agreeing to punch anything and that no one had the right to make him. As Burgess was preparing to answer, Julian hastened to add that he was taking advantage of the opportunity to announce his departure, that he had always hated the company, in large part because of Burgess. With that, he took off his smock, turned on his heel, and left the premises, buttonholing Alfred as he went by.

They found themselves outside under a blazing sun, without any idea of what the future had in store for them and without ever having exchanged more than ten sentences. They went hunting for a location and settled on a disused three-storey building, which they purchased for a song and renovated from top to bottom. The same building where I joined them some years later (at the same time as Simone, I really must mention Simone) and that came to be known as the Icebox because of an association of ideas that no one could miss.

I am still rubbing. The judge is less red but still not at all convincing.

"He's beige now. Stop, Hermann. You've spoiled it."

❧

"You spend every night at the lab," said Clotilde.

"It's the thirty-ninth."

"I would have thought it was more."

It was one of those evenings when I thought I had broken up with Clotilde. I felt like an old story that just won't end. I thought about destiny and I said to myself: maybe, without knowing it, I'm creating obstacles to the one assigned to me, maybe I'm going against my own good, and if that's the case, how can I accept such an aberration? That is, that there are two goods, the one you imagine for yourself and the one you're destined for, and the second one does not correspond to the first. In other words, that there is a superior being who knows better than you what is good for you. If this superior being had decided Clotilde was the right woman for me, he must have been hugely irritated by my insistence on thwarting his plans.

Ten minutes later, the telephone rang again.

"Yes, Clotilde?"

"This is International Cleaning," reeled off a half-female, half-male voice. "May I speak to the lady of the house?"

"Not a chance," I answered. "She just went out."

"We'll call back," said the voice. *Click*.

Twenty minutes later, the same scenario. I grabbed the receiver. "This is the morgue ..."

"Is that you, Hermann?"

A pause.

"We just broke up, Clotilde."

"Speak for yourself," she protested.

"Don't wait for me, okay?"

"Are you angry?"

"Goodness, no, Clotilde. I'm late for a body, that's all. I'll see you tomorrow, okay?"

I hung up. The telephone started wailing again.

"Clotilde, please ..."

"This is International Cleaning," said the eunuch voice. "Has the lady of the house returned?"

"What can I do for you?"

"Spring is on the doorstep," continued the voice.

"It's almost June," I felt I should point out.

"As I was saying, spring is on the doorstep ... going out the door. We clean everything," the voice continued very quickly. "Carpets, furniture, walls ..."

"You're wasting your time."

"... floors, ceilings. Detergent injection under thirty pounds of pressure. Plus softener and anti-static agent ..."

"Oh wow!"

A brief silence at the other end.

"You're calling a laboratory," I explained. "And do you know what we do in this laboratory? We embalm, my dear sir ..."

"Madam."

"We prepare corpses to make them presentable and keep them from stinking until the worms eat them."

"All the more reason," said the voice.

I hung up silently and returned to Germain. He'd been picked up in the park, collapsed on the grass. Solid legs, knotty ankles, hard calves, broad back narrowing at the waist, geometric bodysuit you rarely see on someone over forty. I find it hard to resist comparing their bodies to mine, by turns happy about the flaws I've been spared and jealous of the advantages nature has denied me. I grabbed the calf and lifted the leg. The bones resisted for a moment before yielding. The leg bent silently, the cartilage was intact. Germain was in shape. His muscles had expanded where, and only where, life required it. If Germain owned a car, he also owned a bicycle. In any case, he walked, he had walked. Until his heart stopped.

I heard the vestibule door open and close. Footsteps approached. A woman appeared, armed with a mop and pail.

I exhaled in one breath. "You again?" I almost said, but I stopped myself in time.

"You again?" growled Simone, a succinct expression that summed up the esteem she had for me.

"Hello, Simone. Come on in!"

Simone is our cleaning woman. Transparent from so much washing, dry, and totally sterile. Alfred and Julian take jealous care of her, convinced that she is irreplaceable. Her presence puts me a little ill at ease, so I always treat her with unusual courtesy.

"Would you like to sit down, Simone?"

Which she never does, of course. Partly because the only chair in the laboratory is piled high with books, partly because, and I quote her, the place is "filthy, full of blood and secretions."

It goes without saying that we never deal with the real question, namely, that she is there and I shouldn't be there. She confines herself to tossing something out, a remark, usually disagreeable, or a disdainful look at the laboratory, as if what we do there is indecent. The look she now tosses at me, at the piled-up books and at Germain, lying on the table with his feet open in a V, is as translucent as her skin: "If you read a little less, you could leave a little earlier."

"I'm running late again, Simone."

"I see that."

"Would you like a coffee?"

She looks at my hands with a suspicious eye, as if it is unthinkable that those hands could prepare a coffee that's completely germ free. I know what comes next: nothing. And we both know what the next sentence will be: "I have to clean the labs." Some people, and Julian and Simone are among them, are reducible to a few sentences. They feel it is improper to overuse words and consider the use of substitutes or synonyms an unnecessary expense.

"I have to clean the labs," Simone indeed declares.

"I almost forgot."

A sullen silence.

"We do more or less the same work, Simone. I think we should cooperate with each other."

"Cooperate?"

"Give each other a little more space. I run late, you run late, we run late ... you leave me my lab and you clean the other two."

"I can't."

"Why not?"

"I always start with yours."

Fine.

"It'll take me an hour at most. Then the lab is all yours."

Simone disappears into the room at the back that we use as a kitchen. A moment later, I hear her rummaging in the cupboards. Germain's face is serene. The man did not suffer. A wisp of grey hair lies across his forehead. I push it back. Usually I avoid dwelling on the faces. I could spend hours trying to decipher them. Because while it's true that the body talks to you about its past life, tells you how it has gone through time, the face only tells you one thing: how I died, why I am stretched out here before you. I bend over Germain and pass my gloved hand downward over his face to end all that. It's over, all over, you're somewhere else.

Then I sit down beside him to read a little.

12

The foreman has spent a moment sizing up Number 32 and has told him he will have to wear gloves. The idea pleases him, obviously. A new job with gloves, protective envelopes for his anarchic hands. He mumbles, "Of course, of course," a countless number of times, far too many for the circumstances. Then he grabs the foreman's hand and shakes it convulsively, throws his head back slightly and laughs, he's a pleasure to see.

The foreman is much less of a pleasure to see. He has regained possession of his hand and is sullenly observing the big guy, not at all certain he was right to hire him, but dammit all, aren't they swamped these days? Aren't they terribly short of competent staff? Spring is the worst season for shipping, when they have to make up for lost time after the forced immobility of winter. Compared to those runts with no arms or legs who show up one morning and disappear the next, this strapping fellow might fill the bill. He looks strange, of course, maybe a little simple-minded – why should having to wear gloves make him so happy? – but if you had to worry about everybody's quirks, you'd never hire anyone. He growls, "Tomorrow morning, six o'clock!"

"Of course, of course."

"And don't wear those clothes! You're gonna get dirty."

Yet he had neatly rolled up his long black cape and, not knowing where to put it, stuck it under his arm like a fat, shiny sausage. But he repeats, "Of course, of course," because he's ready for anything and doesn't want to fight with anyone, especially not the foreman, especially not on the first day.

"Uh ..." he says.

"Yes?"

"Roving ...?"

"We service several ports," explains the foreman. "You get to see the country," he adds, trying to smile.

"I see."

"What do you see?"

"It's okay," says Number 32.

The foreman watches him walk away — a stiff gait, arms dangling — less and less sure of having made the right decision. The fact that he laughs for no reason worries him already, and the way he constantly repeats "Of course, of course." Annoying, he concludes.

∽

He takes refuge in the pub. Yseult is there, she's always there on Thursday. The pub is almost full. He goes and sits in the back, as usual. When Yseult is slow to come over, he raises his arm slightly. Yseult sees him; he smiles and draws a huge pitcher of beer in the air.

He watches her walk over with her lithe step, the pitcher in her right hand, a white napkin over her forearm. As she sets the beer down, she brushes his shoulder, he feels her warmth, smells her scent, no perfume.

"How are you doing, Yseult?"

"As usual," she replies.

The kind of answer that leaves him speechless, because he doesn't know how Yseult is usually. She lingers a moment by the table, pushes a wisp of black hair behind her ear, and looks at him, an attentive smile on her lips. Dazed by such receptiveness — the closeness of others always embarrasses and surprises him — he is emboldened and turns his head toward the warmth emanating from her. His eyes reach the level of her breasts; below them, her abdomen rises and falls with infinite slowness. He thinks of a tide, of something warm and moving.

"I was wondering ..." he says, taking a chance.

She makes a barely perceptible movement of her neck,

she doesn't hear well, the hubbub of the voices drowns out Number 32. He clears his throat.

"I was wondering if you would agree to see me … outside," he elaborates with a little gesture that indicates anything outside the café.

"WHAT?"

"I work right near here," he continues, a little louder. "In the port. As a longshoreman. I'd really like to get to know you … for us to get to know each other, I mean."

This time, she bends toward him, unaware of all she's offering in one movement, her eyes, her mouth, her neck, her slightly open blouse. He raises his broad face toward her, could swallow it all in one quick gulp. Her hard teeth that push against the softness of her lips, that nibble, grind, crush … When he opens his eyes again, Yseult is there smiling at him.

"I was wondering if you …"

The rest is lost in the racket of the door opening. The stroke of noon. The bustle of the port that stops and shifts to the cafés, drowning out voices that are trying to make themselves heard and discouraging love stories that want to begin. Yseult straightens up and goes toward them – six men in all, the oldest with a deeply lined face, angular features, a long nose, and a red cotton cap on his head. The man follows her with his eyes. She has thrown the napkin over her shoulder with a decisive, professional movement. Her long black hair hangs down her back.

༄

He doesn't sleep all night. The next day, he reports to the site at five thirty in the morning. Except for two or three employees bustling around, the place is empty. The woman is already on the job, making coffee. He can only make out her narrow shoulders, her bent back, and her neck. He doesn't dare knock, let alone go in, but she turns around just then and comes to the door.

"Coffee?" she asks without smiling.

From the front, she's not as young as from the back. A haggard face, big, pale, dark-ringed eyes. Fifty, fifty-five years old.

"Yes, please," he says.

The door opens and a dozen men make a noisy entrance, laughing and jostling. "Is the coffee ready?" asks Red Cap. The woman shrugs without even looking at him and continues fussing at her two-burner hotplate. The others keep on whistling and making a racket. The woman sets down a huge coffee pot on the counter, with a stack of cups, no saucers, and a mountain of toast.

"Help yourselves."

For a moment, all you can hear is cups clinking and mouths slurping. Number 32 has withdrawn to a corner of the narrow room, his heels, calves, and shoulders glued to the wall. Close physical contact with strangers is unfamiliar to him, and so is this atmosphere permeated with millions of years of dried sweat. They move a lot, give off a lot, spit and sputter a lot, and talk good and loud.

Red Cap turns toward him.

"You the new guy?"

"Yes."

He hands him a cup of scalding coffee.

"Thanks."

"You're coming with us this morning."

He says, "Of course, of course," doesn't ask where or with whom or when or how, swallows his strong, rather bad coffee in one slug as he's seen them do, and chokes. His eyes widen with horror. He gulps air, clears his throat. Bent double, he tries to catch his breath again, but the damned air sacs remain obstinately closed. A man comes over, gives him a hard slap on the back. A violent struggle within, a strong current of air straightens out his alveoli, but he loses his balance. Arms hold him up, dozens of tentacles support him all over, and his face comes up against an overheated wall of wool with an acrid smell. He can't stop coughing and spitting. The wall of wool backs up a little, other arms shore him up. "Come on, fella." He's standing, he opens his eyes and breathes in, red as a poppy, ashamed. End of episode.

Once outside, Red Cap hands him a pair of leather gloves with the palms covered in a rough material. His hands slip into them effortlessly.

13

In the park with Mrs. de Valois. Our conversation the other day has changed our relationship. We're walking on eggs now. It's very slippery.

While setting the canvas on the easel, I make a huge blunder. "It's very impressionistic," I say.

"Impressionistic?"

"It's just an impression, that's all."

"What do you know about Impressionism?"

People are like that. You embalm and they imagine, God knows why, that you're interested in technique. Then I understand. Indescribable relief.

"Is that it?!" I exclaim. "You've finally gone to abstraction? That's wonderful!"

"Abstraction?" asks Mrs. de Valois, more skeptical than I would have expected.

"Exactly, and I'm happy for you, dear madam. It's true, you know! There's no shame in admitting you've taken a wrong turn. Everybody makes mistakes."

She sighs. "I don't understand, my boy."

"Better late than never."

"No doubt, but what's your point?"

"Better the plunge into abstraction than a reality that eludes you. This is an important turning point for you and your career. But think of your public, think of your admirers. For us, it's a real relief. We don't have to rack our brains wondering, But what's she trying to do, anyway? We don't wonder anymore, we just look. And because there's nothing to recognize, we see, necessarily."

"Am I to understand that you like this painting?"

"Absolutely."

"You recognize it, I hope?"

She holds the canvas close to my face and I don't see anything anymore.

"It requires a certain distance to assess a work," I say, backing away.

"What you're saying is very deep."

She backs up too, wielding her canvas like a shield. But from near or from far, I don't see anything. There's nothing more abstract than failed realism.

"Oh yes, that pond again," I say defensively, because I'm not risking much.

"Again?! You're losing your common sense, my boy. That could play tricks on you."

"And there, trees. Or people walking. Unless it's water, it could be water. Trees."

Mrs. de Valois raises her eyes to the heavens, calling on the passersby as witnesses. No luck, not one of them bites.

"I wanted to talk to you about Mr. Hu, Mrs. de Valois. I'm having trouble forming a clear idea of him."

"Is that so important?"

"Oh yes! He entrusted a manuscript to me, his autobiography. I unfortunately forgot it at the greengrocer's stall."

Mrs. de Valois puts the canvas back on the easel and turns to me. "That's certainly very unfortunate."

"I thought I had recovered it all sticky and tattered from the backside of the truck, but it was just an ordinary accounting report."

"I see," Mrs. de Valois sympathizes.

"So I decided to give him a new life. But since I don't have the least idea what kind of life Mr. Hu could have had, I'm asking you. The tiniest little detail would be of help to me. I usually don't have any trouble imagining lives for my dead people. But with the living, I find myself at a loss. And with a living person as discreet as Hu, it's worse."

"Get the neighbours to talk about him, they know. If I were you, I'd crawl on my belly as fast as I could to the

Boisvert-Dufradels'. When you rummage through people's garbage cans all year, you get to know their most intimate secrets. The other day, I had to remind Mrs. Boisvert-Dufradel that recycling isn't a sacrament. She grabs everything I put outside, the bread for the birds, the clothes I hang up to dry. She's already taken two of my nicest slips, not to mention other things. Keep her busy, my boy, keep her busy, it's the best thing you could do for the community."

Just then, Mr. Hu arrives.

"Ah! Hu!" exclaims Mrs. de Valois.

She gives me a conspiratorial little mum's-the-word smile and trundles over to Hu.

"Flower among flowers, I bow deeply to you," says Hu, holding out both hands. "The sun can go change its clothes, you are radiant," he adds in the same breath.

The sky has indeed paled and there are big grey clouds on the horizon.

"Flatterer," coos Mrs. de Valois.

"Admirer," Hu corrects her.

"Good," I feel impelled to comment.

"What do you see there, dear friend of the arts?" asks Mrs. de Valois, indicating her canvas.

"Aha! What have we here?" says Hu loudly, gaining valuable time.

"Well?"

Hu stares at the canvas with a pitying look.

"You recognize it, don't you?" insists Mrs. de Valois.

"Well, you know …"

Hu looks from the canvas to Mrs. de Valois, blinking, as if it's too dazzling for him to bear. "I'm plunging into deep water!"

"If only there *were* any water!" I mutter.

"Go ahead, Hu, go ahead, please."

"Well, I would lean toward … a bison … or a buffalo?"

Mrs. de Valois's legs nearly give way under her.

As shocks go, this was a big one. Flower among flowers was worse than anything I could have imagined. But what is this way of seeing? Metaphor is the sworn enemy of the mortician. The carotid is an artery, the jugular, a vein. The carotid is the entrance, the jugular, the exit. The human body is not a long, quiet river, but a network of more or less clogged channels.

14

He returned home with the gloves. In the entry, he dropped them on the floor, two leather millstones that landed with a thud.

They hadn't needed to fire him. He had left of his own accord, forgetting to return the gloves.

Standing on the wharf, Red Cap had explained his job to him — to unload some thirty small containers that had arrived the day before from Burma — and had refused to let him work at the same time as the others in case there was an accident. "The cables can break, you never know." Number 32 had politely complied. The thick smears of oil on the deck and the drizzle that had been falling since morning complicated operations.

Once the men were gathered farther away for their break, he had boarded the freighter with his stiff, wooden walk and had begun to unload the crates, wondering why they hadn't been put into a single big container and moved to the wharf together. He had suddenly noticed one that was smaller than the others, with the word *FRAGILE* in red letters on two of the four sides. He had stopped and stared at the crate, his mouth twitching. In a flash, the image of his father had come to him, a mere metre forty-seven tall, standing over his petrified figurines like a dwarf king among his subjects, his delicate hands fluttering.

Farther away, the men were smoking, not paying any attention to him, so that none of them were able later to explain exactly how it had happened. All they were able to say was that at a certain moment they had seen the word *FRAGILE* spinning in the air and the big guy catching the crate and putting it down on the wharf as if it were the most natural thing in the world, as if juggling containers were part of a longshoreman's job description.

~

The foreman had wanted to put the interview off until the next day. This was a new situation for him. A guy who throws a container into the air but catches it without causing any damage! If only he had dropped it, things would be clear. He sighs, annoyed. He has no desire to question him about the reasons for his actions. He's not a psychiatrist, his job is to supervise teams of workers, not to try to discover the cause of deviant behaviour. Maybe he slipped, he tells himself, as Number 32 walks slowly toward his office, his long arms dangling as if they weighed a ton. It rained yesterday; maybe he momentarily lost his balance and chose to throw the bloody crate up in the air so as not to damage it, in which case what he did was an act of bravery. He shakes his head, half convinced but more and more uneasy. Should he congratulate the hero of the day or turf him out?

Number 32 gives three little knocks on the door and the foreman, irritated, motions to him to come in. None of my men knock before entering. My office isn't a bedroom, for crying out loud! But he stands up almost without realizing it, an interrupted movement. It doesn't feel right to him to stay glued to his chair in the presence of a person who drinks his coffee without slurping, knocks before entering, and tosses containers into the air.

"I won't be able to keep you on, sir," he says, sitting down again.

He never says *sir*; this too is new. He feels like he's speaking to a crowd, which doesn't help things. To regain his composure, he grabs his stapler and toys with it nervously. Basically, that's the problem, he says to himself. I'm not firing him because of his peculiar way of unloading crates, but because of his *weird-ness*. His strangeness. There, it's been said. He's breathing hard, less and less at ease. I don't like him, because I don't understand him. He belongs to another world and claims to be part of ours.

"Why not?" asks Number 32.

"Your way of unloading is ... all wrong. You could have smashed the merchandise." And trying to soften the blow or to be funny, which he isn't, he adds half-heartedly, "When we say *roving*, it's not the merchandise that's supposed to travel, it's the longshoreman."

"I didn't smash anything."

"I said, 'You could have.' "

The big man lowers his eyes, shaking his head. The linoleum is cracked in places.

"I'm not very muscular," he says slowly. "Maybe that's what you're trying to tell me. In spite of my size and my build, maybe I lack the essential quality of a good longshoreman: muscles." He pauses and sighs. "Pressing keys doesn't require any special strength. Maybe my muscles have melted, which is why you're suggesting that I do something ... different." He stops, confused. "But I didn't smash anything, not a thing."

And then he walks over, grabs the foreman's hand, and shakes it the way you shake an old carpet that's full of dust, puts on the gloves (it's not clear why), and leaves.

15

"Clotilde called," said Julian.

The statement was uttered like a secret. Each word was familiar, it was the whole that hurt. I picked up the scalpel and opened up Lancelot below the navel.

"What time?"

"Five o'clock."

"That's Clotilde. Five o'clock, morning or evening, that's her time."

Julian didn't laugh. Julian is convinced that nothing coming out of the Icebox can be funny. That complicates our relationship a bit, and we leave a lot of things hanging.

"She says you should take care of your cats."

"I take very good care of my cats. That's an oblique way of saying I should take care of her."

"She says they sleep in her bed and it bothers her."

Lancelot didn't have an ounce of fat on him and things went very quickly. Injection, aspiration. Trocar. The tissues were healthy, the outer envelope a marvel. Lancelot had a square jaw, very white ivory teeth, wide-set eyes, high cheekbones, and medium-long hair. All he was lacking, in fact, was a horse and an intact cranium instead of this gaping hole that let you see the grey. Aspiration, injection. The hiss has starting hissing.

Julian, who is not a particularly promising specimen, eyed Lancelot enviously. "Still, he's lucky," he sighed, sending one of those damn brown candies flying.

When I was about to tackle the brain, my hand hesitated. In cases like this, you have to take everything out. I inserted a hook into Lancelot's nostril and pushed. It found its way easily. Julian was holding the head.

"Still your old Egyptian methods!"

"You can't stop progress."

The brain always catches me off guard. That mass shining like a concentration of energy.

"I find it indecent to take the brain out through an open wound surrounded by bone fragments," I muttered. "Besides, Lancelot's whole life is in there," I added in one breath.

It was one of those mornings when I felt a strong need to vent. I would have dropped everything, I would have taken Julian to the café, and I would have said to him, just like that, point-blank: "Where do ideas come from, Julian? And what use are they? What use is Zita? And what are dreams? Illusions? Secretions of our desire to change the course of events? What do we morticians do with them? Do we destroy them with everything else? Do we flush them down the sewer with the blood?"

"You should break it off," Julian said.

Alfred and Julian are both married. To them, anyone over fourteen who's single is oversexed or searching for himself. I don't think I'm the former, and if I'm searching for myself, what am I supposed to do about it?

"You ought to settle down once and for all," Julian added. "You always seem like you're somewhere else."

"Somebody has to be there. It's crazy all the people who are here."

Lancelot was running out, his youth, his good and bad deeds, everything he had been, collected in the steady flow of grey thought pouring out patiently, inexorably, while a characteristic sickly sweet smell gradually filled the room.

Alfred came in for the second washing. Alfred is the great expert in second and third washings, and when I talk about a third, I'm serious.

"Clotilde called."

"So I'm told, yes."

"Clotilde's very nice." His tone was curt. "Why don't you stay with her and work in the daytime, like everybody else? Simone complains that you stay late at the lab."

Silence.

"She also says she doesn't feel at home here anymore," Julian added.

"Simone certainly tells you a lot. No danger of that happening with me."

"In the evenings, the labs are hers," continued Alfred. "They're her domain in a sense."

"Domain? Did she really say *domain*?"

Alfred retorted, "Do you know how long it takes to find someone who's willing to work here?"

"She hasn't left, as far as I know."

"The smells, the bacteria, the risk of contagion ... Dammit, Hermann!"

Alfred, Julian, and Simone share a hatred of bacteria. When it comes to asepsis, they're a formidable trio. Alfred was talking in his crazy way. Julian came over, crushing some of his candies underfoot.

"Let it drop, Alfred."

"Let it drop? They only come because they don't have anything else, you know as well as I do. When they're not afraid. When, by some miracle, and I do mean miracle, they pretend they're not afraid, they have to be trained."

"Don't exaggerate."

"I'm not exaggerating. It's hell here. The minute you step out the door, you're responsible for everyone. Responsible for the baker who touches you when giving you your bread, responsible for the butcher, the cashier, your wife, your children ..."

Alfred lost his youngest child. After the day he let a woman in here. His wife.

"Calm down, Alfred. I'll talk to Simone."

His wife had arrived unexpectedly, young, rosy, buoyant. The wind had blown her hair back.

Alfred was washing Lancelot.

"Stop now, he's clean."

She had placed her precious bundle in her husband's arms.

"Calm down, please. We're old hands now."

"I'm always afraid."

I took Alfred's hands and held them in mine for a moment.

"Every day it's the same," he moaned. "I wash my hands fifteen times in a row. I wash them, and then I wash them again. Look."

"No need."

I knew them by heart. Two swollen mauve things with blue veins.

"We'll do it together for a while, okay?"

His eyes misted over.

"What do I look like, for God's sake!"

"Nothing at all, Alfred. If you want, we can start over again."

"Like an alcoholic."

"Only for a while."

I led Alfred to the sink and washed his hands gently, I simply let the water run, I rubbed but not hard. I talked to him as if to the child he no longer had. "Wash them again," Alfred said each time. "No, Alfred. They're clean now." "Okay."

"We need a cleaning woman, Hermann. We need Simone."

"Yes, Alfred."

"The interns will be arriving soon."

"Not for several weeks."

"The labs will have to be cleaned."

"We do it every day."

"Simone does it. But what if she isn't here anymore?"

"But she is here."

"And there are those damn candies. Those brown things Julian drops everywhere."

"You think so?"

"You're so absent-minded, Hermann."

⌇

"Get the neighbours to talk about him."

It's very simple, it seems like no big deal. But it has something journalistic about it that makes them clam up. The day before yesterday, I walked out of the building and ran right into

Mrs. Delpèche, and no doubt Mrs. Lenoir too. Two witnesses in one shot. I should have been doubly happy, but instead I was doubly perplexed. Mrs. Delpèche has a yellow complexion and orange hair, which means I have no idea how I should act with her. As for Mrs. Lenoir, her contours are not clearly defined. You get the painful feeling of having before you an emanation of intangible particles that the slightest thing – a breeze that's a little bit strong, a persistent rain – would be enough to topple into nothingness. To gain their trust, I brought out my good old greetings, one of the best being:

"Hello!"

I sensed no openness, only a kind of glum discomfort.

Mrs. Delpèche replied, "Hello, hello," a disturbing redundancy that might suggest she was storing up a reserve so she wouldn't have to greet me the next time we met. Mrs. Lenoir, in a particularly volatile mood that day, placed herself behind Mrs. Delpèche, which more or less transformed her into a halo.

So I decided to try Mrs. Boisvert-Dufradel, because of the affinity that had developed between us with the retrieval of the tatters, and so that Mrs. de Valois would stop losing her slips. I put on my most recyclable jeans to knock on her door.

Mrs. Boisvert-Dufradel looks me up and down, with a long pause at my jeans. One of the Boisvert-Dufradel kids is hanging from her skirt, a sort of shiny throw that would be more in place on a couch than around her waist.

"They've seen better days," she says, looking at my poor jeans. "What are you waiting for to recycle them? They'd be more in place as insulation in a barn or on the seats of my son's pants."

"No, please," interjects the son in question. "I don't want them."

"He doesn't want them," I say.

He raises two shy eyes to me, wrapping himself in the thick folds of his mother's skirt.

"It's more and more of an uphill battle," Mrs. Boisvert-

Dufradel sighs. People buy cheap, tacky things, then they throw away more and more, but what can you do with junk?"

I could almost sympathize. After all, we had one thing in common, the absolute certainty that the end was not final, that you could always make something out of it.

"Speaking of which," she continues, "I wanted to ask you, what do you do with your dead bodies?"

"I beg your pardon?!"

"All that unused material! Why incinerate or bury it when so many things could still be useful?"

"We already do that," I mumble. "Some give their eyes; others, their kidneys, their livers ..."

"Is that all?"

I was starting to get excited. "Do you know that some people categorically refuse to part with even a single hair on their heads?"

"A total lack of environmental consciousness!"

"Integrity is a right, madam. So is not recycling."

"Recycling is a duty, sir. Even a low-life like Hitler understood that!"

Even without my fainting, she realizes how inappropriate that is.

"Because of your work, I'd have expected you to be more daring, and since the other day, I thought you were won over to the cause. You move heaven and earth to recover a bunch of useless paper from a garbage truck, but you can't be bothered to recycle your dead bodies."

"It was an autobiography, not a bunch of useless paper!"

"So you're writing your life now?"

"Certainly not!"

"Was it an autobiography or not?"

"Yes, but not mine."

"Whose was it, then?"

I had already said too much. Mrs. Boisvert-Dufradel looked at me with huge scandalized eyes.

"You threw somebody else's life into the *garbage*?"

"Not at all. I forgot it at the fruit seller's."

She made an odd movement toward me, kind of a sudden leap, which threw the little Boisvert-Dufradel off balance.

"It's yours, isn't it?" she whispered with a smile that revealed most of her teeth.

I shrugged two embarrassed shoulders.

"You're keeping secrets! Come on, stop being so timid! There's no shame in writing your life."

That all depends on the life, I thought. I imagined the one Mrs. Boisvert-Dufradel would write, a daily routine filled with discoveries and recoveries, each one more surprising than the next, a life regulated by the rhythm of garbage collection, with unspeakable periods of boredom.

"And in a way, writing your life is recycling. Since it's no good for anything anymore, you pass it on to other people."

She let out a big hearty laugh that shook her from head to toe. It shook her balcony too, and the birds took off and the kid fell to the floor.

"It's not my life," I said. "It's Hu's."

She immediately calmed down.

"Since I lost it, I have to reconstruct it and rewrite it. I came to ask you if you knew anything about him, what he threw away, what he recycled."

"Are you telling me you're going to write what *really* happened in Hu's life? Because I'll have you know there's no question of letting the whole building find out about my relationship with him. And besides, can you really call it a relationship? A few moments of folly around the municipal dump. Because he followed me, you know? I had seen signs of his interest in me, but I would never have imagined that ... Anyway, I mistakenly believed that we shared a passion for recycling, but that wasn't it at all, not at all."

The words were uttered in a tone of indignation.

"It was false, all false! Once the process of seduction has begun, you know very well, there's that most painful time when you feel you're being pursued like a cornered doe ..."

"What's a corner doe, Mom?"

"That doesn't concern you!" snapped Mom.

He had finally managed to get up and was keeping a cautious distance.

"So, after that first test every woman who's at all interested in the opposite sex is subjected to, I saw very well that it was nothing but hot air, his supposed interest in me, in what matters to me."

I was trying so hard to put Hu and Mrs. Boisvert-Dufradel together, I don't mean in the same bed but in the same room, that I was having a lot of trouble following her.

"I'm not the right person to ask. I very quickly put a stop to Hu's pathetic efforts. Ask the others instead."

"The others? What others?"

"The others, what others! You sound so young! The other tenants, of course!"

"But … they're all 110 years old!"

"He still doesn't get it! They haven't always been 110 years old."

Until that moment, Hu had been nothing. Suddenly, he not only had a life, but a *sex* life.

"Could you be more specific, Mrs. Boisvert-Dufradel? I mean who, in particular, may have had a close relationship with Hu?"

She pursed her lips for a moment and turned toward her son, which seemed incongruous to me.

"Well," the son answered immediately, "there was Mrs. Delpèche, there was Mrs. Claire, the one who takes baths, Mrs. Gertrude too and then …" He shrugged. "As for the others, I don't know. I only know the ones who did it in the daytime. At night, I was asleep."

And to think that all this time I had felt I was on safe ground visiting one or another of the tenants, never suspecting that some of them had an active past. I thought of the old Scout. Maybe he too, under the harmless exterior of an intrepid Otter, was sexually active.

"And Mrs. de Valois?" I asked, my throat dry.

"Oh no, not her. She'd rather paint."

"He has an incredible memory," she said, smiling.

She observed a moment of silence, a welcome silence that allowed me to reorganize my muddled neurons, and then she came and stood in front of me and looked me right in the eye.

"And what do you intend to do with your drafts?"

16

He has made coffee and is drinking it in cautious little sips so he won't choke·like the other day at the port. The half-dozen newspapers bought at the corner tobacco shop are lying on the table. He goes through them one after the other, patiently, especially the classified ads, trying not to give in to despair. He has a certain sense of humour, but he observes that it fails him just when he needs it most. Today, for example. No matter how many times he tells himself that his situation is exceptional, that it's not every day you run into an Artistic-Realistic-Enterprising pianist who's a former longshoreman with blocked alveoli, he doesn't find it at all funny. I haven't taken the time, he says to himself. There's a gulf that forty-one years haven't been able to fill. This spring with its constant rain and those wet trees whose leaves are struggling to open and unfold, I haven't looked at them enough. The leaves will reach their maturity without my knowledge and will form their complicated lacework without me. Not to mention all the rest, the rest that is everything. Love, affection. He doesn't speak the word out loud because he knows that if he does, the walls will come tumbling down. It's too big, too great. And now, I'm this stammering person: "I would like to get to know you. I would like." He's standing beside his piano and bowing, his left hand wide open on the glossy black surface, he's always made that gesture, with his hand designating his soul. He is the one being applauded, but it's thanks to the piano that people are standing up to applaud him. For being the one who gives, the bringer of joy and dreams, but whose hands have evening after evening crushed his own joy, his own dream.

This morning, they're looking for an assistant beautician, an apprentice tinsmith, a serviceman's helper (to serve the serviceman), a professional accountant, and a pet sitter. It's better than yesterday. Yesterday, they were looking for a plasterer, a part-time drywaller, a carpenter-ant exterminator, and a DJ, an abbreviation Number 32 didn't understand. At the very bottom of the list, his eyes have fallen on the word *piano*. In the grey mass of typographic characters divided by headings, his attention has been drawn downward toward those five letters: *P-I-A-N-O*. He contemplates them for a moment, amazed and filled with sudden gratitude, and he feels the air entering his lungs again, dilating them to infinity until they encompass the totality of the known universe. His universe. *Upright piano player wanted to entertain our distinguished clientele at La Chenaie Community Centre.* He raises his head and looks outside. The day is grey, still no sun. What exactly is a community centre, and where is La Chenaie? Why do they specify an *upright* piano player? A pianist is a pianist. And what is the distinguished clientele before whom he would have to play? The man sees pearls, solemn, wrinkled faces, imposing chests. And above all, what would I play for them? What do distinguished people like? Ballads? Well-known melodies? I don't know any. And I'm not the entertaining type.

He goes over and sits down at the piano to play some scales, but his thumb rebels. His index and middle fingers press down the *D* and then the *E,* and the thumb starts to move behind the fingers to land on the *F*. But there's an intolerable fraction of a second, a delay imperceptible to any ear but his. A note that is delayed and disrupts the precious balance.

He starts over ten times, a hundred times, and spends the whole morning at it. He stands up, enraged, and slams two impatient hands down on the keyboard, and the old Steinway groans. He grabs the pair of gloves, rushes past the row of unopened medications, and goes out.

~

He is in front of the rather ugly modern yellow brick building, 72 des Échelles Street, the address on the brown envelope. There are people coming and going. Two closely entwined young people wearing identical jeans and jackets come out. They stop two steps away from Number 32 and kiss for a long time, so long that he's suddenly embarrassed and he lowers his eyes and stares at his shoes. He would like to move, to get away, but he's afraid of attracting attention. The door opens again and two old women stick their noses out, their bodies half inside with the top halves flung outside to inhale and assess the heat, the cold, the tepid, fearing one as much as the other. One of them decides to come out, she's almost there when a tall, wiry man in navy shorts and a white cap boldly pushes the door open, nearly knocking down both old women.

Their appearance has given the signal for an exodus. Other ladies, more or less old, more or less able, come out in turn. Backs bent, shaky arms leaning on canes or walkers. So it's here, the man thinks. He makes a quick calculation and wonders how old his mother would have been, whether she would have been that fragile, that impermanent. He sees himself looking after her, visiting her once a week on Sunday, bringing a box of chocolates. Would she have been able to walk without help, would she still have had her wits, would she have had a dog like the one with that fat, short-legged woman wearing a sack dress that goes down to her ankles? A gentleman emerges behind them, a slender greyhound with a fluid gait who hurries past, greets them briefly, and heads off as he always does, as he always has done.

The man turns away, short of breath. So this is where he lives, he says to himself. Here, in this village of old people. Such a concentration! And this life, in spite of everything, this life! The slender greyhound has just crossed the street. The man follows him with his eyes, thinking of his mother, of her absolute solitude. He thinks of Yseult, who has never seen his house, of the upright piano and of the unknown well-known melodies.

"Excuse me, sir."

He starts, then steps to one side. Another lady, younger but prematurely wrinkled, is looking him up and down without warmth.

"I have to take out the recycling bin, you're blocking the way."

The word offends him.

"I'm not blocking anything, my dear lady, I am here, that's all. I have to be somewhere."

The lady doesn't laugh. She's younger than the others, it's true, but her little washed-out face does not stand out among those hollow, fleshless masks. He yields nevertheless.

"Forgive me."

How many times has he yielded this way, how many times has he spoken those words? The earth is made for middleweights.

17

The door opens. Mrs. Claire is in front of me, rosy, perky, and superclean. Behind her, the reassuring gurgle of a bathtub emptying.

"Oh no," she says. "Not this time! If the building is taking on water today, it's not because of me."

"That's not why I've come."

She opens the door wide. "What can I do for you?"

"You can give me some information on Mr. Hu."

I give her the least detailed account possible of my misadventure.

"And why have you come to me?"

"They mentioned ... they told me ..."

"Who are 'they'?"

I wave my hand vaguely toward the outside, in the direction of the Boisvert-Dufradels' apartment.

"Oh! The Dufradel kid?"

"That's right, yes."

"And what did he tell you?"

"Uh, well, that ... that you were friends, or that you had been."

"We still are."

"Friends in the other sense."

"We're no longer friends in that sense."

"Hu must have confided in you, told you about his life in China."

"In China? As far as I know, he's never set foot in China."

"Really?"

"He was born on Descôteaux Street, right near here."

"Ah!"

An absurd question comes to me: if you were born on Descôteaux Street, why would you write your life story?

"What about his parents?"

"Third-generation immigrants. If you're looking for something picturesque or exotic, I'm afraid you won't find any trace of it in Hu."

"But he must have had a desire to retrace his origins, to go back to the places where his ancestors were born?"

"To hear you talk, I almost wish he'd done that. It would have made our conversations more stimulating. No, in fact, Hu isn't interested in those things." She gives a quiver, a weary shrug of the shoulders, an old movement that takes the place of laughter. "To tell you the truth, Hu is interested only in two things."

"Really? What are they?"

"Women and miniatures."

"What kind of miniatures?"

"All kinds. Paintings, objects of all kinds. Hu loves anything that is radically and resolutely small. Almost obsessively, I'd say. Come have a look."

I follow her into the living room. Lined up on the mantelpiece are what at first I take to be bits of broken glass. A huge pitcher would have provided just about this quantity of shattered glass, but it would have taken a madman to line up the pieces with such care. They were microscopic sculptures of incredible refinement. Leaning closer, I saw that they depicted animals, some familiar — elephants, camels, monkeys — and others rare — demons, dragons, and other rather formidable creatures.

"He gave them to you?"

"For every birthday," sighed Mrs. Claire. "And every time he comes here, he lines them up again in case I've moved any. As if I could have moved them! I can't even see them anymore. My eyes are not so good now. And since I don't see them, I end up dusting the miniatures when I dust the shelf. It's lucky I can still find most of them, and as for the rest … The other day, I had to rummage through the garbage cans to retrieve them. Mrs. Boisvert-Dufradel was there too, of course. The trouble I had getting them back!"

She shakes her head in discouragement.

"In fact, that's what drove Hu and me apart. He only likes what's infinitely small, delicate, imperceptible. How can you expect a woman to stand up to such demands? I need expansiveness. Anyway, it's been a long time since I set foot in his place. To be precise, since the day I unfortunately sat on his collection of Persian miniatures. I didn't do it on purpose! I thought they were part of the pattern of the sofa. But who says he wrote an autobiography, anyway?"

I think again of the twelve manuscripts on my night table. Still, I can't reply that autobiography is an obsession of golden agers.

"Who says his book wasn't just an essay on miniatures?"

Just?

I have to close my eyes at the thought of what awaits me.

"I'm sorry I can't tell you more about him. Look into the miniatures. That's the only thing I remember about him." She pauses and then shoots me one of those looks I really don't know how to respond to. "Actually, no, that's not *all* I remember, of course not." The smile again, the shudder, the face glowing with happiness.

"His skin," Mrs. Claire murmurs. "The beauty of his skin. You can't see it now, but it really did exist. Talk about the miniatures and the softness of his skin." She looks away toward the window. "His skin, and that way he had of ... of entering me." She gives a little cough. "I know, it sounds banal. But not all men proceed in the same way. With him, it was ..."

My eyes are quicker than hers, they flee to the window, a neutral place where there's no risk of seeing Mrs. Claire and Mr. Hu locked in an embrace. Why this embarrassment? I wonder. What's so hard about it? Mrs. Claire has a heavy, stocky body dressed only in a wrinkled little cotton dress that could have passed for a tablecloth. She had just gotten out of the bath and had tied up her hair in an indescribably thin little bun from which two or three colourless wisps escape. There's no comparison with Mrs. de Valois, who carries her corpulence with a rare elegance. Mrs. Claire is hardly pretty and has probably never been, but she has the soft, dreamy quality of people who have loved life. Not necessarily all of life, not necessarily all the time, but once, on a certain day, at a certain time, she said yes to what was offered her and revelled in it.

"Hu was a decent man, an art expert, not very imaginative perhaps, but a decent man. We were friends, yes. For many years."

"Tell me about his life. Was he married? Did he have children?"

She comes back to me almost reluctantly.

"He was a curator for several museums. I think he's been married, but I'm not sure. Ask Mrs. Delpèche. She likes everything official."

"What do you mean?"

"Well, she also had a thing with Hu, there are several of us, you know. But she's the kind of woman who doesn't jump into the water without making sure there's a raft, and if possible a freighter, waiting there in case of a disaster. There's probably nothing she doesn't know about Hu."

She looks me straight in the eye and then I see what Hu saw and what touched him, no doubt. Mrs. Claire's gaze did not brush over you, it ripped you out of the ground, worked you over from top to bottom, and tossed you back on the shore. It didn't make you feel unique or precious or greater, it confirmed your existence, good or bad.

Mrs. Claire carefully closes the door behind me.

18

"It's been ages," murmurs Antoine.

The two men look at each other in silence. Antoine has aged. So has he. But he's put on weight, Antoine hasn't. Slim and as lithe as he was at twenty, as he must have been at thirty, and as he will be at sixty.

"Fifteen years," says Number 32. And because artists, especially out-of-work pianists with Parkinson's, have time to count (unlike overworked producers), he adds, "Fifteen years, seven months, to be exact."

He had finally decided. To get up, shower, dress, leave the house, go knock on the door at Art Music, a record company run by Antoine Ziegler, and although Antoine is an old friend, to prepare a little speech explaining that he had never dared to tackle Ravel's Concerto for the Left Hand but that he feels capable now at forty-one, a mature artist at the height of his powers — and with discordant fingers and joints in knots, but that's not part of the speech. He had made an appointment, not, as one might think, to be certain he would be received, but so that Antoine would have time to get used to the idea. Looked at this way, it's pretty frightening.

He had been invited in and asked to wait. Not for a long time, just enough to show that they were swamped but were making time for a friend, what wouldn't they do for a friend?

Antoine had given him a hug. A nice gesture, certainly reassuring, but suspect. Such a warm reunion after years of silence! Resigned, stiff as a board, the pianist had waited for the other man to release him from his embrace. Over Antoine's shoulder, his eyes had met those of the secretary, two narrow slits in which surprise vied with duplicity and expertise acquired through long experience. Antoine had ushered him into his office, shooting a glance toward the narrow slits and tapping his watch. In a quarter of an hour, make up some pretext, anything, so I can get rid of this! A quarter of an hour! The message is clear, the secretary is used to this.

In the office, Number 32's gaze falls on the pile of magazines on the desk. Normal, he thinks. Art Music must subscribe to everything about music.

"Have a seat."

Which he does, his heart pounding, a little bit impressed in spite of himself. Same office, new furniture, all chrome and glass. Twenty-two years earlier, he'd come here for the first time to imprint the mark of his talent on vinyl. He was nineteen.

"We never see your name anymore!" exclaims Antoine, indicating the pile of magazines in front of him with his chin.

We never see your name anymore, no one talks about you anymore, everyone has forgotten you. He hadn't thought it would come so fast, this introduction of the subject that feels like a verdict being delivered. His throat tightens, he swallows painfully. Twenty years have been enough, he says to himself. Twenty years have been enough to perfect this strategy as smooth and pitiless as the blade of a knife.

"Don't tell me you read that stuff?" he says with feigned assurance.

"I read everything that allows me to keep in touch, to keep up with things," Antoine declares calmly.

"And to turn down big artists on the way out who come asking for help from a friend."

It was the right thing to say. You can't block all the punches and Antoine Ziegler was not prepared for that one.

"Is it my fault if you're losing it?"

Number 32 takes the blow without raising an eyebrow. Only his hands move. As if warned of imminent danger, they flutter on his knees, and he buries them quickly between his thighs like wriggling puppies.

"You produced my first five records. You and I in a sense created Art Music, with me playing and you producing."

"And you leaving Art Music, me continuing to keep it operating. Alone."

"So? You've done pretty well for yourself."

This time, it wasn't the right thing to say. Antoine reacts as if he has been insulted. His body gives a start and he squints his eyes.

"You don't just drop the company that made you famous," he says curtly.

"All artists do. They become well known and they get invited to tour and cut records. Elsewhere."

"Some come back, as surprising as it may seem. Some stay loyal to those who gave them their start."

Antoine stands up and goes over to the window. From the back, he looks even more severe. A sleek head on top of absurdly straight shoulders. Handsome, certainly, but stiff, contained, constricted, sweating blood for years to maintain his appearance, with the same absolute discipline that has allowed him to make a name for himself and bring everyone remotely involved in music to his company. Outside, it's a beautiful day, the sun is gently drying the gleaming patches left by the recent rain. When he turns around, the pianist is still there looking at him, his unseen hands sheltered in their vise of warm flesh.

"I don't want to rehash the past, it was forgotten a long time ago. I'm not going to take you back, but it's not because of that. You know very well why."

He leaves the window and comes to stand in front of Number 32.

"It's been years since you've done anything good. You stopped at thirty-six. I've been following your career, I'll have you know."

"Thirty-six!"

He tries to remember what he was like at thirty-six, what he was doing that year, that day, the day he stopped, apparently. Was it fall? Was it spring? Was the weather good? Bad? He has a tender thought for that person who lost everything at the age of thirty-six, who came and went, strolled the streets, eating and digesting, without suspecting the monster that from one minute to the next was going to throw itself upon him and drag him down. He looks down at his hands quietly intertwined, the left one holding the right one still. He knows that if he frees them, they'll take flight like two impatient birds.

"Which means I'm no good for anything anymore."

Antoine objects, "I didn't say that!"

Number 32 stands up too and leans his tall body toward the other man. "How dare you judge my talent? How dare you say I stopped at thirty-six?"

Antoine feels the warm breath on his temple and backs away. "It's my job, believe it or not. You only have to compare. Listen to your recordings and compare, buddy. Anybody could tell. Anybody."

He sways, his suddenly freed hands gesticulate, his big legs buckle. Antoine holds him and prevents him from falling, as the wall of wool soaked in male sweat did the other day. He extricates himself with a shake and straightens up. "And you?!" he shouts. "When did you stop?" Words pour out, not those prepared for the occasion, old ones that have been waiting a long time and that he has never spoken out loud.

Then he calms down, makes an effort. "You're wrong. Everybody's wrong. I can still do it and I'm the one who decides, not you. Not 'anybody,' as you say."

"But I'm the one who pays."

"Of course."

He turns away, defeated and oddly relieved. The way you are when you've lost an important competition and you know there won't be any others. At least I didn't shake his hand, he thinks, there's that much. He opens the door and walks away without a misstep and without turning around, alone, to face what will come. The two slits follow him.

"I can't stand the idea of you touching his body."

He's not even thirty years old. As soon as he sat down, he'd leaned toward me as if he wanted to share a secret. His raincoat is soaked and he hasn't even taken it off. "A body is not something you can manipulate," he says in a low voice.

The other one, the one that must not be manipulated, lies beside us in the refrigerated drawer. He's even younger.

"If you touch the body, you blur the image. I don't know how to say it."

"I understand."

"Do you believe in eternal life?"

"I would like to. The last lap is sometimes hard."

He hesitates. "What I'm asking you to do is illegal, isn't it?"

"Yes. In this country, embalming is mandatory."

He puts both fists over his mouth and closes his eyes. I wait. I can't do anything for him. Suddenly, from the street, we hear the clear voice of a child: "Daddy, did you go get my dog?" "Not yet," answers another voice, soft, a little weary. "Oh!" says the little girl with annoyance. "You have to go! Now!"

He has buried his face in his hands and he's crying. It could be him, I think. In another place, other circumstances, that young man, tired but happy to go get a dog for his daughter's birthday, could be him.

"I won't touch him," I say.

He remains motionless, as if he hasn't heard.

"I will not do what you don't want me to do."

19

The water is flowing in abundance.

I'm bent over a body, any body. Zita is breathing on my neck. I can barely stand other people's breath because of the false warmth and the reek of acidity.

"I can't work with you so close to me."

She walks around the table and stands facing me. "Explain it to me …"

And I explain. "We always start by washing the bodies …"

My voice has the slightly solemn tone of a Sunday preacher making his first appearance on TV. Zita's there, with her long, supple body and her multipocket jumpsuit embellished with countless zippers.

"It's a long operation, but absolutely necessary. For external asepsis, do you understand?"

Then the image dissipates, the presence vanishes, and my heart is no longer in it. I think of fall, which will come in its time, I think of Zita, who will come in her time, or won't come. I think of October, I think of my excitement. My lips open and I say, "Zita, Zita …"

༄

"You're talking to yourself," says Clotilde.

She's waiting for me in the next room, the bedroom. With the cats. I come out of the shower, dripping, I want to collapse. Clotilde watches my every movement.

"I have something to tell you."

"No hurry, we have our whole lives."

I lie down facing the wall. For the close-up and the lack of perspective. Some nights, I don't want to see farther.

"It can't wait. It's about the two of us."

"You're asking the impossible."

"We're stagnating," says Clotilde.

I take a deep breath. "It's what we do best, and at least we're doing it together."

Something rises very softly and comes toward me. The futility of what we are.

"Don't block me out completely," murmurs Clotilde.

I turn toward her. I see her eyes in close-up, her beautiful brown eyes misted over. "You're too close, Clotilde."

"That's because you're too far, Hermann."

We're face to face, our features wan and drawn. The thanklessness of age. Clotilde has lowered her eyes and is contemplating her hands. The room is full of tensions, some resolved, others that will never be. I think about feelings and about their range, which is huge. In the multitude of emotions experienced, there was surely a place for Clotilde and me, and what I felt for her, something that perhaps had no name, that wasn't called love or friendship or intimacy, or anything, a new, original feeling that would concern only Clotilde and me. For a moment, I accepted the absurd, the unimaginable, I renounced Zita, her presence on my neck, her breath, her voice, and all the energy her absence demanded of me day after day.

Now only Clotilde and I were in the bedroom, her hesitation, her hands that opened and closed for no reason, her sorrowful face leaning over our raft bed. I stretched out my hand to her and stroked her cheek. My heart started beating again as it always does, out of time. Clotilde smiled.

"It's so noisy!"

I took her in my arms and held her tight. She was stiff and disenchanted. Her arms, dangling at her sides, had already given up. I squeezed harder, until I felt the warmth rising again within her and mixing with mine, until her arms finally came to life and encircled my body like two forgiving branches.

~

In the park again, the same park. Mrs. de Valois's gaze flits from me to the pond. The same pond.

"It will be harder than I thought, I'm afraid."

"Why is that?"

"Well, because I don't have much to work with. Mrs. Boisvert-Dufradel threw in the towel after the preliminaries with Hu, and Mrs. Claire only remembers the softness of his skin and the way he had of ... no, never mind."

"Of what?"

"Well, it seems he had quite a unique way of entering."

"I can't believe such a thing," protests Mrs. de Valois. "Hu is no burglar."

"I didn't mean entering in that sense, I was talking about ... Did you know, he was quite a success with women?"

"No, I didn't know. Good Lord, which women?" To hear her tell it, the women in question could only have been Martians or mentally deranged.

"Mrs. Claire also says Hu is an expert on miniatures and that the autobiography may in fact be an essay on them. It's all rather depressing."

Mrs. de Valois suddenly straightens up. "No more depressing than having someone tell you they see a bison where there isn't the tiniest hint of a bison," she says drily.

"People close to you are not the best judges of the merits of a work," I suggest to get her to relax and stoop again. Seeing her all straight like that when she's usually at an angle is making me uneasy.

To create a diversion and bring things back to me, I say, "I'm afraid of missing the essential."

"If I were you, I wouldn't worry too much about it," murmurs Mrs. de Valois. "Managing to see a buffalo in one of my canvases shows a flagrant lack of artistic sense or, at best, a senility that neither you nor I would dream of describing as premature."

Had I seen something worse than a buffalo in Mrs. de Valois's canvas?

"You see? That's the problem. The more questions I ask, the more different opinions I obtain about Hu. Where's the truth in all this?"

"The truth, oh my!"

"You're a painter, Mrs. de Valois. You have the power to establish the truth, to reproduce what is. Don't let such an opportunity pass you by."

"What do you mean by *reproduce*, my boy?"

"Imitating what exists or has existed; it depends," I say patiently.

She takes the trouble to put her brush down, which is no small matter. "That's not what I'm trying to do."

"Why not? What do you have against reproduction?"

She doesn't hesitate a second. "Nothing. But it's of no interest."

She looks so sad that I deduce that she has hurt me.

"To me," I say, "it's not at all without interest. Reproducing is a noble act. I think seeing things as they are requires a certain courage."

"Of course, my boy. Of course."

"Being a painter can be that, too."

"Not always. It all depends on what you see. We don't all see the same thing."

"That's very dangerous."

"Why is that?"

"For consensus."

"What consensus?"

"If everyone sees what they want to see, it's war. There's no agreement possible."

"That's not true."

I feel very hot all of a sudden. "I can't accept that."

"Can't accept what?"

"All this ... relativity. I hate randomness. You have to call things what they are. A cat is a cat, or Sully or Théo, because everything has a name, you know, everything has its designation."

"Calm down, child."

"I'm not a child. You know that perfectly well."

"It's a figure of speech, nothing more."

"I'm extremely attached to words. The truth must inevitably come from there, and I think that what is said will one day be heard."

"But words have more than one meaning," Mrs. de Valois insists. "They say something else. And that's what you're doing yourself."

"What?"

"Misusing words. That's all you do, I'd say."

"That's not true!"

"Oh yes, I assure you."

A man passes with a triple stroller carrying triple progeny. He slows down as he passes the canvas and gives me a huge wink, indicating Mrs. de Valois.

"To me, the important thing is to show what has been. That's what the survivors want, that their dead be recognized. If they are no longer seen, if no one recognizes them, what's the point? Don't take that away from me, okay?"

"It's not my intention to take anything away from you, my boy."

Mrs. de Valois's hand lingers on my shoulder.

"Because I'm a useful person. I sincerely believe that."

She nods yes, but at that age everything moves, you can't tell anymore.

"More useful than you, at any rate. What use is a painter who refuses to reproduce?"

"None. Why do you absolutely want to be useful?"

"Because, after all, being useful is existing. How do you know you exist if you're not useful for anything? It's like Zita. Does she exist? Right now, she's of no use to me, which means I am constantly in doubt. She comes and goes in my head, sometimes stays, sometimes doesn't. A bit like me, but without the cushion."

"Usually I manage to follow you, my friend. By concentrating a bit. Who's Zita?"

"A former intern."

"And what else?"

"A woman I liked."

"Oh! And you're worried because of your friend Clotilde? She's a nice woman, Clotilde."

"That's what I think too."

Since I don't add anything, Mrs. de Valois speaks these words, which warm my heart: "Would you introduce me to Zita?"

"I'd like to, but I would have to get in touch with her. The first steps are more than I can handle."

"Oh!"

"There's nothing harder than calling someone you think you love without being totally sure and without knowing if she corresponds to the image I have in my head, and, most of all, without knowing whether or not she wants me to call her. Probably not, anyway. Alfred and Julian, especially Alfred, always say that in love, everything is decided in the first forty-eight hours, a view I certainly do not share, by the way, since my reaction time is always slower than other people's ... Aren't you going to say anything?"

She comes closer to me and her smell changes the atmosphere. "I'm trying to untangle all this. I'm not young anymore."

"I've always thought that, because of the work I do, because of being with the dead so much, I might be better than most people at seeing beyond appearances, which would only be fair. But, to tell you the truth, I'm not so sure. I'm not at all certain, that's what I'm trying to say."

"I think I understand."

"You're there with your intuitions, your confident words, but there's no one more dubious than a doubting mortician."

The next minute, she's hugging me, rocking me, and murmuring strange things. Her hair is very close, her heart is pounding, mine contracting.

And what about our conversation?

20

"Listen to your recordings and compare, buddy. Anybody could tell. *Anybody*."

Anybody, who exactly is that? he wonders as he walks along beside the park. The pedestrian hurrying toward me? The policeman directing traffic? The mother who just let go of her child's hand and turned around, confused? Or the odd fellow gesticulating in front of the painter with the tractors, the unnerving bionic reader with the divine hands. Twenty-six seconds. He was 17, and I, 32.

He stops right in the middle of the sidewalk, forcing the people behind him to stop short and go around him. He retraces his steps, goes into the park, spots a bench, and drops onto it. The drizzle has gradually changed to rain. The painter with the tractors is hastily gathering up her things, assisted by Number 17, who takes off his jacket and covers the lady's shoulders. With the canvas and the easel wedged under his left elbow, he slips his right arm under the old woman's arm and leads her, taking careful little steps. So many precautions, thinks Number 32.

He follows them with his eyes for a moment, unable to move or turn his attention elsewhere. Once the pair is out of sight, he leans back on the bench. Could he express an opinion on my music? he wonders finally. He sees the full silhouette again, the shoulders sagging under an invisible weight, the light brown hair that grows low on the neck. Would he have that particular talent of being able to say yes or no, it's still okay or it's not anymore, it was better before, it's just as good today.

Anybody could tell.

It's raining hard now. His eyes riveted on the deserted bench, he merely turns up the collar of his jacket. And while the park empties, while mothers call their children home with loud cries, while lovers laugh and raise the flimsy shelter of their damp clothing over their heads, his body curls up in a long, slow movement, closing around itself, spine curving, knees pulling up to the stomach, the primal body become one again, round, impervious.

21

"He's been married twice, he has a child from his first marriage, he's worked in at least four museums, I can give you the names if you like but it would take quite a while to find them and I don't think it would be relevant."

Mrs. Delpèche stood in front of me, stiff and yellow, haloed not by Mrs. Lenoir but by a strong aura of permanent. Her erratic orange hair was congealed in a web of tight curls. Broaching the subject had been relatively painful; that is, I'd had to explain, which meant admitting I was in the wrong. I'd bet that, in her whole life, Mrs. Delpèche has never forgotten any manuscripts at a fruit and vegetable store.

"Beyond the description of events, I would like to know what is the essence of Hu."

"What essence are you talking about?"

"Well, what distinguishes one person from another, what makes them unique."

"Because you think Hu cared about his essence? Hu was not unique in anything, at least not to me. He was like all men. He was the third one to promise to marry me and not keep his word. You'd think that a man capable of blindly committing twice before wouldn't have balked at a third marriage. But no!"

"But you had a very close relationship with him …"

"What do you mean?"

"You shared your life with him, you confided in him and he in you …"

She exhaled suddenly as if the air were polluted. "What you're describing sounds idyllic."

"I can't fill two hundred pages just with what you've given me."

"That's your problem, not mine. I gave you all the stages, you just have to fill in the gaps. Elaborate, for goodness' sake!"

"I'm told he liked miniatures. Do you think the autobiography could be something else?"

"Like what?"

"An essay on miniatures, for example."

She pursed her lips in a skeptical pout. From all directions, an army of wrinkles attacked the mask like so many arrows pointing the direction to go. "I doubt it."

"Tell me about the son."

"He lives in the north end of the city, not very far away. He's a musician. A pianist, actually, I think."

"What's his name?"

"Hu."

"Have you ever met him?"

"Never. But I know he exists. I checked." And seeing my shocked expression, "What do you think? That I was going to marry Hu without knowing who I was dealing with?"

"Good Lord!" I said, very much in spite of myself.

"What?"

"Nothing. But how can someone want to control things to that extent? I'm sorry to say this, I didn't come to say this to you, I'm not trying to offend anyone. I'll leave you now. Can you be discreet about this? Don't say you'll be as silent as the tomb, okay? Any other word will be okay."

"I'm nothing like a tomb, I have a dreadful habit of talking without rhyme or reason to everybody and anybody. The proof is the son. Admit that sometimes shrews like me have their uses. Isn't that true?" She smiled. Nothing trembled, no birds took flight, but the air all around us began to breathe.

I lifted Balthazar's head to clean the back of his neck. Then I straightened up and looked out the window. The streets were dark and gleaming with rain. It was suffocatingly hot inside and out.

I picked up a second cloth to wash his legs. His skin was black and smooth, almost hairless. My hand slowly moved up from his knees to his groin and then back down to his feet. My movements were marked by contemplation and the ease that belongs only to seasoned professionals or innocents, the quiet assurance that makes you want to touch flesh, dead or alive, the assurance that is in fact love, that brings bodies together before conscience puts up its wall of prohibitions between them.

Suddenly I felt very alone.

22

I rang twice, and made a point of going back down the six front steps each time, for distance and out of respect for privacy. But no one came to the door. Maybe he was out, maybe he was eating, it was only five thirty, but it's true that some people eat in the middle of the afternoon.

I was about to leave, unhappy and frustrated, when the door opened slightly. At first, I couldn't see anything. Then I made out a half person, a shoulder, part of a face, and an eye, moving, slightly slanted, sunk deep in the socket like a trembling old wolf.

"Sorry to bother you, I'm looking for Mr. Hu."

"That's me." His eye stared at a point in the middle of my person. "To what do I owe the honour?"

"Your father entrusted me with the manuscript of his auto-biography, which I wish to rewrite since I lost it at a fruit stand."

The right eyebrow rose very slightly, I don't know about the other one.

The door opened suddenly and I saw the other half. Square face, thick hair, long nose, fleshy mouth. The body was in keeping with it. Massive shoulders, enormous arms, swollen red fingers. Altogether, he looked kind of Neanderthal.

"Who are you, exactly?"

"I told you, I'm the person who lost your father's manuscript. It was by questioning the neighbours that I became aware of the existence of a son. I did some research in order to get in touch with you so that you can help me fill in the gaps, because I figure that if anyone knows the father, it must be the son. I intended to phone you before showing up at your house, but I just can't bring myself to phone, you see, it's like with Zita, I just can't do it, so I came here to try to meet you, since I know practically nothing about your father except that he likes miniatures, that he had beautiful skin, I say *had* because now it's a bit wrinkled like everybody else's, and that he gets into people's places without breaking in, but I didn't mean to disturb you, perhaps you were cooking your evening meal, it's not the time, I admit, but it takes all kinds to make a world."

A justifiable moment of surprise. Then, "This way of expressing yourself, what is it exactly?"

"A fruitless attempt to embrace the world in its totality."

"You've come to the wrong place. My father and I are hardly in contact anymore."

"Oh!

"But I was indeed about to fix myself something to eat. Come in."

I hesitated.

"When it comes to cooking, I do pretty well," he insisted. He straightened up. "And I always eat alone."

The entry was small, austere, and empty except for a wooden bench under which an array of huge shoes was lined up, as if a family of giants had taken them off on entering. To the right of the entry was the living room, to the left, the dining room, and straight ahead there was a narrow hallway to the back of the house.

There were delicious smells emanating from the kitchen. I have unqualified admiration for people who are able to marry edible substances, to transform a vegetable as innocuous as a cabbage or turnip into an appetizing dish. Who was the first to think of combining pork and sage? I see nothing obvious about it.

So I witnessed the marriage of pork and sage. Hu handled the ingredients with ease.

"I really want to rewrite his book," I felt I should remind him.

"What makes you think he wrote his autobiography?"

"Nothing, but I assume it. I already have twelve lives on my night table. Why would your father be an exception?"

"Why would he have entrusted it to you?"

"Because I read a lot and because I live in the same building as he does."

"Are you friends?"

"Not exactly. In fact, I daresay your father and I don't have much in common. He misuses metaphors like nobody's business and his lack of understanding of modern painting is shocking. Believe it or not, he mistook a pond for a buffalo, not to mention everything else."

"Is he senile?"

"Not in the least."

"But why are you interested in him?"

"Because I lost all trace of him, I told you."

"Trace? What trace?"

"What trace! His, of course. It's what you leave behind when you depart this earth. It's all that's left of him, that trace."

The wide mouth stretched and stretched, and a kind of growl came out. "As far as my father is concerned, that is certainly not all that is left of him. If you want my opinion, he's been leaving his trace just about everywhere."

That was also what Mrs. Claire and the Boisvert-Dufradel boy had implied. Hu certainly scattered himself.

"He's old," I protested feebly.

"My father has only one passion, as you said." He was looking at me, I've never had anyone look at me like that, greedily, the way an entomologist looks at the insect he's about to pin in his box. "A passion matched only by his aversion to anything bigger than three and a half centimetres. Unfortunately for me, I've never been three and a half centimetres, except in my mother's belly, if then." He gave a big hearty laugh, the kind of explosion that catches you a little off guard. "Tell me about yourself instead." Return of the entomologist's gaze.

"I work in a mortician's laboratory. My father would have liked me to be a doctor. A mortician, you have to admit, is a notch lower."

The pork and sage were celebrating in the frying pan. Hu busied himself at the stove and I could see the curve of his back, which was huge, and his oily hair. The image of the father appeared before me. His elegance, the extreme slenderness that could be taken for refinement if you were absolutely certain that the two went hand in hand. Hu, mobile, nervous, slim, beside this huge strapping fellow whose fingers, I'd bet, extended way beyond the edges of the narrow ivory keys of his piano.

"Did my father ever talk to you about me?" asked Hu.

"We don't talk very much, you know."

"But enough for him to entrust his autobiography to you."

"You're surely in it."

"A mediocre pianist whose career ended at thirty-six," Hu reeled off as if he were reciting a lesson.

There was a heavy silence, broken only by the crackle of the meat in the pan.

"Judging oneself is a hazardous undertaking," I said.

"Nonsense! No one is a better judge than oneself. People know perfectly well what they're worth. You know it too. Besides, you absolutely reek of success."

I would have liked to reply, Where do you see that? but I knew the answer. I said, "Mediocre in the old sense of the word, then. Average."

Hu dropped into a chair, and everything suddenly became ordinary again. A second chin appeared below the first, his hands at rest looked like two big clenched claws emptied of their prey, and his two upturned feet, like a pitiful pair of parentheses bracketing emptiness. "I know what is beautiful, you see? Few people can boast that talent."

He lit a cigarette. "I've tried them all. All the pianos, one after the other. For a while, I thought they were to blame, they weren't worthy of my talent. Now I know that no piano in the world will be able to give me what I want." He inhaled deeply and coughed, the smoke took forever to come out. "When I sit down at the piano, I know that anything can happen, that there are no limits set in advance. But when I get up again, I know it hasn't happened. The idea inside is too high, I can't live with the disparity."

Hu crushed his cigarette as if he had a grudge against it and looked me up and down. "What about you, when you work, what is it you're looking for?"

The question took me by surprise. "What do you think," I stammered, "what could someone who empties and fills bodies all day long be looking for?"

"I don't know."

"I'm looking for … what isn't in front of my eyes, what is never given to me. I'm looking for what always comes to my table too late. I think you know what I'm talking about."

He was making an effort to hear, but his eyes had already left me, the entomologist had left his laboratory, the insect remained alone in the darkness of its box, pinned there forever. "What I'm looking for is God," he declared calmly. "When I play, I *am* God." He lit another cigarette and smoked with his fingers spread and the cigarette very close to his mouth.

"There's such violence in you," I said.

"We must not accept trivial talk."

I got up to take my leave. I was in the way in the kitchen, I didn't know what to do with myself, and especially with him. I headed toward the front door. The house was completely silent, and probably had been since the beginning, but I felt the absence of noise for the first time, it had become palpable, a substance, a material I could have touched by reaching my hand out. The house was neither beautiful nor ugly, neither old nor young, it was the house of a person who thinks of only one thing, whose entire universe is reduced to a single striving.

"You're leaving already?" Suddenly, he was there beside me, distressed.

"I don't want to bother you anymore."

He didn't understand.

"I won't achieve anything with my attempts at reconstruction. Your father had his own life, but it doesn't seem I'll be able to draw anything from it for the time being."

"So leave my father where he is."

"That's what everyone tells me. But that won't get me anywhere."

He had turned on the light in the entry and a bleak yellow glow came down from a brass sconce high above, giving us both hollows as deep as ravines under our eyes.

"Stay," he said.

"Why?"

"We haven't had anything to eat yet."

"I'm not a great success with the living, you know."

"Then you've come to the right place."

Hu turned the fire off under the pan, took out two plates and two glasses, and set everything down on the table. He opened a bottle of wine and we ate in silence. There was no awkwardness between us, I ate as I would have eaten alone, he drank without looking at me. From time to time, he seemed to remember that I was there and gave me a quick glance in which there was fear mixed with a kind of recognition.

The time passed in this way. Without exchanging more than three words, we together got through that fateful period, the low point at the end of the day when just about everybody, even the most fun-loving person, even the most outrageously happy, gives a thought to oblivion.

At one point, he said, "Do you think I'll make it?" He was leaning toward me, his body was like a big ship out of water, a ship that has finally let itself run aground.

"No, probably not."

He nodded in agreement.

"I'm sorry."

I chewed and I watched him drink in dainty little sips like a cat. I said, "Don't die, please."

That was the moment life chose to manifest itself. It's the last thing you expect when you work in a mortician's laboratory. You're there with your stiffs, you're manipulating dead matter, you know what's to be done, you're used to it, ready and willing, and *wham!* life pops up again just when you're not expecting it anymore, with its hummings and its voices from beyond the grave.

" 'Scuse me ..."

I had just washed him, I had towelled him off, I was about to sit down and read by the window. I had tucked his feet under the towel so they would dry on their own. Then I had covered him with a sheet, for modesty. My book was straddling his left kneecap. The action was placed in nineteenth-century Sweden on a farm that had been passed down from generation to generation, and for reasons it would take too long to go into here, sordid plots were afoot around the inheritance of the farm.

I was working, as usual, bent over the sink. And all of a sudden, behind me, the soft swish of naked flesh against naked flesh.

" 'Scuse me, sir ..."

Something fell to the ground with a sound like dead leaves.

The farm! The Swedish farm has fallen to the floor!

I don't turn around, no, I only look up at the wall and try to understand what's happening. The laboratory is empty at this time of day, Simone isn't here yet, and the corpses don't talk, at least not much. I close my eyes and try to swallow normally.

"Sir ..."

I sniff the air and I finally understand what's been wrong since the beginning: the air is not heavy, the air is unchanged. Dying involves a change in smell. The man behind me gives off an odour of whitewash. Plus, the corpse is soft, not the least bit stiff and never has been. I'm going to pass out. I give a thought to my father, my father who wouldn't have let a live one get away for anything in the world.

I still hear the warm rubbing. My immobility is total, my hands are icy. I say, "Good afternoon."

I should have said *good evening*, since it's evening, but behind me, the voice answers obligingly, "Good afternoon."

Then I turn around. He's leaning on one elbow, his eyes surveying the room. The sheet has slipped down, revealing a pudgy white shoulder.

"Let's remain calm, everything's normal."

"What happened to me? Did I have a blackout?"

"*Blackout* is a very big word."

"What's the matter with you?" he asks me. "You're white as a sheet."

"I could say the same about you, sir."

"And why are you trembling like that?"

"The cushion. It's the cushion."

"The cushion? What cushion?"

"How do you feel?"

"I feel queasy. What am I doing here?"

"There was a system failure."

"In my system?" asks this Lazarus worriedly.

"No, the big system. The signs were misinterpreted."

He's more and more worried and I can only agree whole-heartedly. "But seeing you here beside me and alive means that I haven't done all this for nothing, that death can be reversible and that Zita is possible."

"What's Zita? A tornado? A germ?"

"More like the first."

"And why would it be reversible?"

"I said *possible*, not *reversible*."

"This obsession with naming everything these days! And where am I? In a hospital?"

"Not really."

"A clinic?"

"You could call it that."

"What's it going to cost me? Clinics are usually private, they cost money."

Strange, really, how quickly human beings get back on their feet.

"Nothing, nothing at all."

"Where are the nurses?"

"Out."

"All of them?"

I pretend to check my watch. "Simone should be here before long now."

"Is Simone the nurse?"

"You could say that."

The man sighs, and I do the same. I feel hot.

"I think I'll leave," says the man.

He sits up and laboriously stretches a foot to the floor. The table is too high, it wasn't designed for someone to get down off it. With the movement he makes to stand up, the sheet falls and reveals his plump nakedness. The man doesn't seem overly concerned, he looks at his hands, his wrists, as if their nakedness was more compromising than his overall lack of clothing.

He observes me with an overtly suspicious eye. "My watch? Where's my watch? And my wedding ring? Where's my wedding ring?"

"With your loved ones, I would imagine."

He throws his shoulders back. The hairless roundness of his belly, inconspicuous in a lying position, is pushed forward.

"Why do I have nothing on? It's freezing in here. Where are my clothes?"

"Behind you, sir. Hanging on the hook."

With a dazed look, he contemplates his very sober black suit. "That's my Sunday suit," he says. "What's it doing here?"

"It's quite simple, sir. Usually, people who come here leave more stylish than they arrived. It's a matter of decorum."

The man frantically grabs clothes and throws them over

his privates. "I'm in a madhouse," he says very softly, as if he didn't want to hurt me. "The emergency ward was full, so they sent me here, right?"

Fortunately, I'm a rock, with all the experience I've acquired over twenty years, otherwise I might have taken that the wrong way. He's clearly a sensitive person.

Without taking his eyes off me, he starts to dress, with movements I can only describe as rushed. "Turn around," he orders. "It's not proper."

I turn to the wall where the instruments of death are displayed, and I suddenly feel like exploding. With joy. I stammer, "What did you see?"

"What do you mean, what did I see?"

"See, yes, feel. You must have felt something?"

"You mean when I passed out?"

"Passed out or passed over."

"Nothing at all. I saw nothing at all. Was there something to see?"

"The long tunnel, the moment when everything is illuminated, your life flashing in front of your eyes like a long ribbon ..."

Behind me, there's silence. But life is doing its work, I can hear it. The rustling of clothing has replaced the swish of flesh, the movements are maddeningly ordinary. I hear the shirt being hastily pulled on, the zipper jerked up, the shoes put on. The man is quick and efficient. I feel his eyes on me, don't turn around or else ... How does he see me? What will he say about me? Some poor nutcase talking about a tunnel and a ribbon.

"Make an effort, would you? Try to remember."

What follows is quite horrible: Simone makes her entrance in an aura of antibacterial perfume. She opens a mouth completely empty of sense.

"Hello, Simone. Come on in! Have you come to clean the labs?"

"Is that her?" asks Lazarus.

I nod, smiling, because everything is true to form and predictable.

"The nurses do the cleaning here?"

"Diversification of tasks, yes. To vary their work and break up the routine. Right, Simone?"

Her mouth remains obstinately agape.

Lazarus gives a quick little bow. "Evening, madam."

And, contrary to all expectations, Simone reacts. With nothing in the man's words to justify such a reaction, her complexion goes from clean white to a rosy red that heralds joy. Her mouth abandons its downward curve and the atrophied corners turn up slightly. The zygomaticus major and minor very nearly go into action. In the memory of mankind, the Icebox has never before known such excitement.

"Okay," the man says, heading for the door. "So that's that. I have things to do."

"Are you leaving?" asks Simone abruptly. Three words that are worth their weight in gold, three words never before spoken, three words that reveal the unsuspected richness of Simone's vocabulary. But it should be remembered that for Simone, leaving is at the top of the scale of human virtues.

"They must be expecting me," says the man soberly.

"That's far from certain," I say.

"What do you know about it?"

"You should phone first."

"What time is it?"

"Around nine, nine thirty. Something like that."

"Perfect. There's no danger of waking them up."

He bends down to pick up his necktie, which has fallen on the floor, and walks past me without another word. What happens to the dead who don't die, God only knows. This is not an exit worthy of someone who has experienced a miracle.

I go to him. "Take care of yourself, sir. I don't want to see you for at least ten years. Ten years is very elastic."

A dismayed glance in my direction. I have an irrepressible urge to give him a hug.

"There were butterflies of all colours," he suddenly declares. And since I don't react, "Your question before. There was actually a little blackness, but not more than when I close my eyes."

"You should see your doctor, just in case."

"Why? You're a doctor, aren't you? With all due respect, the less I see of you, the better I feel."

My right eye catches Simone, who's putting her hand over her mouth. I can already imagine her telling Julian and Alfred that I was having a conversation with a false dead man.

He nods, walks past Simone, who's standing at attention holding her broom, and slows down.

I say, "You're immortal, sir. It's up to you to stay that way."

And then he goes out, and then he's gone. And I find myself alone, face to face with a pink and perky Simone.

"An event like that doesn't happen every day, Simone. I think we have to be able to accept the extraordinary."

She's already in the kitchen. It's an aspiration of hers not to remain in my presence for more than thirty seconds in a row. I follow her, of course. I have no idea how she'll react. How does a fossil react to the unbelievable? Simone is sitting facing the window with her back to the door, her right arm resting on the table, and her fingers are running up and down the neck of a half-empty carafe. How old can she be? What is her life like outside the Icebox? Her fingers are still brushing up and down against the glass in a continuous movement that indicates boredom as much as irritation. Or sex. But short of being depraved or abnormally imaginative — and God knows I'm neither — it's impossible to associate Simone with sex. Simone does not and cannot have the slightest sexual connotation. Except that her hand continues, the movement has its effect, and I dread the moment when the glass will explode in front of my eyes.

The body moved by Simone's innocuous action.

My gaze leaves her hand and moves up to the areas of Simone that are less fraught with consequences, the back of her head, her very straight spine, her bent neck, and the bone that sticks out beneath her immaculate collar. On the table, beside her hand and the aforementioned carafe, a small snack wrapped in aluminum foil. No cutlery or plate, nothing but that shiny crumpled foil that reveals a glimpse of a slice of cold meat that has not yet been bitten into. What would Simone's body, half hidden under the table, be like?

"I have to leave," I say. As if she were keeping me, as if I were spoiling her pleasure. *I have to leave.*

I back out of the kitchen. I turn around only when my back bumps into the doorframe, and I leave the Icebox, slamming the door behind me.

～

On the way home, the memory of the resurrected man flooded back. Simone really had spoiled the miracle for me, but then it sprang up like a geyser, filling me with a joy that is impossible to describe but that arises whenever the inexplicable bursts into our lives. Going back home, I ran into Mrs. Boisvert-Dufradel. I grabbed her around the waist, and kissed her on both cheeks. She smelled of unscented Marseille soap.

"They don't all die, believe it or not! Some give up, some change their minds, irreversibility is an illusion."

"That's what I've been trying and trying to tell you, but you refuse to believe me."

Since such great effusions are brief, I put Mrs. Boisvert-Dufradel back down on the ground. She was red and a touch congested. She sniffed the air.

"What's that smell?"

"Pure soap."

"No, on you."

"Oh, that? It's nothing. A cat. Found it on my way home."

"Your cat stinks."

"It's dead."

She backed away.

"I'm planning to embalm it in the ancient Egyptian way."

And because I was in a teasing mood that night, I added, "I'm a generous guy, you know, I'll give it to you. I had intended to give it to Simone, but I'll give it to you. You'll probably be able to do something with it. Cats can be recycled."

She refused outright.

～

The next day, I brought the cat to the lab. It was a small male, thin and recently deceased. Working on the head, I saw that there was a hole in the skull. The bullet had gone into the eye – the brain had run out through the socket – and had lodged under the right axilla. The animal had been shot at point-blank range. I imagined the scene: the cat cornered at the back of a squalid yard, the crouched body seeking a way out and not finding one, the crazed eyes, the horror, the fraction of a second when it understood.

The profession I practise is conducive to melancholy.

24

The operation took me about an hour. The cat looked just about the same as when it was alive, even better. I laid it out in plain sight on the windowsill, across from the door. Simone saw the cat. She immediately reported the thing to Julian and Alfred, who, God knows why, deduced from this that I was overworked.

～

"Simone says it's not sanitary," Julian protests feebly.

"We don't embalm cats!" Alfred adds curtly.

"Sanitary? You think *she's* sanitary?"

"Well, yeah," growls Julian. "You can say what you like about her, but you can't fault her for not being sanitary. It's her main virtue."

"You should get some rest, Hermann," Alfred concludes.

He gives Julian a sidelong glance and Julian returns the look.

"She also says you've been coming on to her."

"Nonsense!"

"That you've been ogling her like she was a beauty queen."

"You're sort of at the end of your tether," Alfred says. "With everything that's been happening to you!"

"Well, it's not my fault if the dead refuse to die."

"No, but the publicity is bad for us."

"The publicity? What publicity?"

"Hermann! We've made the headlines for the past week!"

"So? It brings in customers. It's reassuring to see a funeral parlour detect life at a glance. A company that was less professional and more expeditious than ours would have embalmed the gentleman right away."

"Even so," says Julian. "The family is suing the doctor."

"So what do you want me to do? Finish the guy off so the doctor doesn't get in trouble?"

"No, but ..."

"But what?"

"You didn't have to bawl out the doctor too."

"I got bawled out. By the whole family."

"You have to understand them, Hermann."

There's a silence and the three of us look at each other, happy but doing everything possible to hide it. Lazarus changed his will and designated the Icebox the heir of two-thirds of his estate. Alfred and Julian suddenly become serious again.

"How," sighs Alfred, "does a simple mortician manage to get into such a predicament?"

"I'm not just a simple mortician."

"You need to get some distance," suggests Julian.

"Go away for a while," adds Alfred.

"The ICCM starts next week ..."

They are silent long enough for me to digest the information. The International Congress of Certified Morticians takes place every two years. I would resort to anything to get out of going.

"Alfred and I have unanimously designated you to represent the Icebox."

"It's not my turn."

"It's been your turn for years, you skip it every time. This year, you're going."

"I hate conferences."

"Long enough for us to forget the incident."

"And for Simone to recover," adds Alfred.

"You're going," insists Julian.

"I'm totally useless in that kind of meeting."

"We don't give a damn."

"I hate speaking in public, I have very little feel for communication, I stumble over my words, I long ago gave up on developing my verbal skills."

"Play dead, then."

Hilarity from my two associates.

"You'll have some fun ..."

"... and so will we, at the same time."

"Good Lord, it's a conspiracy."

"Absolutely."

There are no dumb jobs, there are only absurd jobs. Making clean what will a moment later be soiled gives the illusion of life to matter destined for putrefaction, preserving what will be destroyed, it's Sisyphus endlessly rolling his rock up the mountain.

We practise the art of likeness; that is, the art of the fake, of artifice. Making it look as if nothing has changed, as if they were sleeping, as if at a certain point they felt tired and simply lay down for a nap. But no one is fooled. They have good colour and a smart look, but that's not them, certainly not, it's not them. It's not him. Did he ever look so ill at ease, so placid, he never crossed his hands that way, his lips were never fused, sewn up, or glued. In the worst moments of doubt, they had that amazing capacity to open up, to shout to their heart's content, but not here. What is this taut body, this obscene standing at attention? He was warm, he was supple. How does this mummy ease the transition to death?

We work on appearances, on illusion. But why is the illusion of reality so essential to us? Why not reality? Most people spend their lives wanting to be different from what they are. So why not give them that last tribute? Why not ask the dying what they would have liked to be and turn them into Superman, Beethoven, Einstein? Why not give them what they never had? This soul that refused to surface, let's create it from scratch; this beauty to which they aspired, let's invent it for them.

25

Any participation in a meeting of more than two people is an ordeal for me. When the meeting brings together more than 150 people in the same profession as mine, the ordeal is unbearable. Usually, this type of event is a kind of party, an opportunity to get together with colleagues, to talk syringes and cannulas, to have a laugh and a few drinks. Not for me. Progress only has a moderate appeal for me. Past civilizations have expounded enough on the subject of death that we now have a right to take it easy and not look for problems where they don't exist, and I like to believe that, today, in our changing modern societies, there are questions that have been settled once and for all and don't require analysis, study, reinvention of the wheel, rationalization, or reorientation.

It should be clear that my presence at the ICCM won't do anything for anyone and that my role will be essentially passive, if not to say silent. I won't even accept the status of observer. A person who observes makes some kind of effort that commands respect. I don't observe, I see, because I can't do otherwise, and I hear, because I'm not deaf. The only thing I do at this kind of event is attend. Conferences have the huge advantage of making you experience time differently; everything is so long and boring that time becomes an eminently concrete thing. The most ordinary, the most insignificant second that goes completely unnoticed in the hubbub of daily life is suddenly endowed with unsuspected duration, with a beginning, a middle, and an end. You watch it pass the way you watch a train pass, see it coming from far, stretching out, leaving again, immediately followed by the next one, and so on.

Still, I wait. People, actions, movements strike my retina, words enter my auditory canal. Three-quarters of the time,

I just sit there contemplating my peers, my brothers, wondering what I'm doing here when I should be reading beside my dead.

∼

The conference was being held in an old inn that was actually called The Olde Inn. It was located in a village on the bank of a river that must, in its time, have provided a watery view but was now reduced, no doubt because of global warming, to an insignificant and rather foul-smelling creek. The Olde Inn, too, must have seen better days. Today, you could criticize it for just about anything but false advertising. You were struck at first glance by the dilapidation of the premises, not to mention the hydroelectric facilities. The shower provided a stingy stream of water, the bathtub drain was blocked, and the bedside lamp switched on only every second time.

The conference was to last three days and the theme was "Green Disinfectants: How to Sterilize without Polluting?" It opened with a series of welcoming speeches followed by a reception, where I passed the time counting the men and women. There were two women for some 154 men. The profession is attracting more and more women, but they had apparently decided to pass on the conference this year. Rather than strolling nonchalantly from group to group, glass in hand, saying hello to people as if I knew them all by their first names, I stayed close to the raw vegetables, because that was still the safest place to be.

No need to add that the cushion was there and played its protective role as never before.

∼

The closing dinner was trying. Wedged between a fat man who guffawed at all his own jokes, drafting me as witness to their drollness, and a very young, freshly graduated pastor who was there to see with his own eyes "these men and women who are totally dedicated to the preparations for the final journey," I spent two interminable hours wishing with all my heart that I were somewhere else.

The man kept laughing and telling joke after joke between mouthfuls, and as a result, his mouth was almost constantly open. Since the air could not properly oxygenate his lungs, our man would stop at regular intervals and noisily clear his throat to expel the excess carbon dioxide and then start up again with renewed vigour.

"Believe it or not, he was ready to do anything to recover his wife's diamond. There he was, sitting in front of me trying to convince me that the ring was only of sentimental value to him but that it was the last remaining thing of hers and he wanted to keep it. Sentimental, my eye! The diamond was at least one carat, or something like that."

I knew all I had to do was turn toward him, which I wouldn't have done for anything in the world, to see his tongue in action, the mashed-up food against his palate, the fillings in his molars, everything you should avoid looking at if you're tired and if you want to continue believing in the greatness of humanity.

"But there was no way to get that damned diamond off! The lady was swollen, her ring finger had almost doubled in size."

He laughed even more before revealing the end of the story, which was predictable and quite pathetic. "I acted like I didn't get it, of course, until he started to talk about money. Then I acted like I was horrified, the persnickety type. He piled on the cheap sentiment, upping the ante. I gave in."

"And?" asked a guest across the table.

The man grabbed his knife and pressed it against his finger, pretending to cut it off in one quick, precise movement.

"And how much did you get for it?"

"Two thousand!"

"And what did you do with the finger?" I asked, less out of curiosity than to stir things up.

"I put it in the casket with the rest," sputtered the man.

To my right, the young pastor who had come to see these men

and women who were totally dedicated to the preparations for the final journey was starting to fidget. Sitting across from him, his wife kept opening and closing huge green eyes with long black eyelashes, as if she were trying to dissipate a bad smell.

I turned to the clown. "The reverend here and his wife are no doubt starting to wonder whether you're joking or serious. Reassure them, for pity's sake. Explain to them without delay that the deceased have rights, and that those rights are clearly spelled out in the mortician's code of ethics."

I felt sick to my stomach and there were sharp pains in my back. Close by, I sensed movement. Someone slipped in beside me. I knew right away that it was a woman because only a woman can slip in like that. I smelled her smell before I saw her. This woman was embalmed in the noble sense of the word: a slight citrus fragrance, nothing heavy, no roses or chrysanthemums, nothing like that. Light. The fragrance was light.

I opened my eyes. The woman was leaning toward me and looking at me, smiling. Her eyes were hazel, almond-shaped, with clearly defined tear ducts. In comparison, her mouth seemed small. Her lips were substantial and devoid of makeup, with a slight downward line that indicated that this woman was experienced.

Since she had slipped in first, it seemed fair that I start the conversation. "I'm glad you're here, I didn't know how I was going to get out of a tight spot and I was about to toss aside my ideal of civility, which I generally consider very important for life in society."

"I've been watching you since the beginning," said the lady. "You're so different from the others."

"It's very kind of you to have noticed me, usually I'm abysmally transparent. As for my being different ... do you think I don't look like someone in this field?" It's always a pleasure to be told you don't look like your occupation.

"On the contrary," corrected the woman with hazel eyes. "You're the only one here who looks like an undertaker. Really, look at them, do you find them credible?"

It was true that they didn't look serious. Because of the late hour, they had taken off their jackets and loosened their neckties, and their overall attitude had something relaxed about it that was far from proper, at least for a mortician.

"The fact is, if I were dead, I wouldn't entrust myself to them," I said.

The woman looked at me and moved still closer. Given the tiny distance that separated our two selves, I could see the moment when I wouldn't be able to answer for my actions. Because I now have a confession to make: she had something, this hazel woman. Other than her big brown eyes, other than her mouth that was fluttering two centimetres away from mine, she had what you call presence, and I'm not made of wood. Anyway, if I compared her to the other women at the meeting – that is, the only other woman, the one with green eyes and black eyelashes – she won hands down. I didn't understand very well what was happening inside me, I was a knot of conflicting, confused feelings. But I had only one wish, that the hazel woman would stick to me like glue and would make a new man of me, a man who would give up sterile waiting and seize life.

She must have sensed my confusion because she came even closer. "Do *you* feel like staying here?" A sentence fraught with meaning and addressed to me personally, since the *you* was in italics.

I suddenly felt very hot. "This kind of get-together is known to be an opportunity for illicit affairs. Please, let's not prove the cliché true. Let's behave instead like true professionals sharing a common ideal."

"But I have no ideals," replied the lady. "I have no profession either. I have no reason to be here, I came with my mortician husband."

"That's a little like me. I'm here myself only as an imposter. I mean, I'm not the one who should be here, but rather Julian or Alfred, it was their turn, not mine, mine should have come later, in about fifty years, especially since I hate meetings like this, where we haven't learned anything much since the

Egyptians, meetings where you have to dialogue, where you deal only with side issues such as natural versus makeup and never the real problems like spontaneous resurrections. That happened to me the other day, a poor devil who had been put on my table without having died, which meant I had to set the record straight, to talk him out of it, and that led to all kinds of more or less suspicious negotiations."

She was there beside me, her one and only activity consisted of being there beside me and looking at me. Plus she was beautiful.

I surrendered. "Take me away, please, I don't have the strength to take myself away."

She was full of life and radical decisions. She jumped at my opportunity and surreptitiously slid her hand under my forearm. Her warmth irradiated my skin as if no clothes separated us, true intimacy. We stood up in a single movement without any consultation or strategic planning. I believe I bade farewell to the guests who were still hanging on. My former neighbour with the excited jaws had moved to the other end of the table and had already begun serious preliminaries with one of the waitresses, a young woman with long thin legs and red hair. The thought that he and I had something in common, illicit preliminaries, a lapse, bothered me, I confess. Had I known that we actually had something else in common, I would certainly have dropped our plans.

I thought of Clotilde, Zita, and others who trusted me. I had drunk and conferenced, which I wasn't in the habit of doing. I'm only trying to explain something that happens to me rarely, the sudden desire to feel my hips clasped by a pair of thighs, a desire for female closeness, for a lack of spaces, for forgetting, basically, for forgetting.

It's an understatement to say we threw ourselves on the bed, it was the bed that came to us even before we had touched the door and awakened the lock with a trembling, awkward key.

In the dim light of the room, her skin was the warm colour of copper, the light washed over her like a wave over a beach of red sand, and her epidermis wanted nothing better than to drink it all in.

We undressed by mutual agreement. She ran her hand over my naked thigh as if she were checking its solidity. Her hand came and went on my skin like waves of affection and desire. I yielded to the extravagance of the hazel eyes and I melted into her with my body erect, my joy complete, and my soul athirst for this fateful moment that would not soon come again. I drank as I had never drunk, I inhaled what she offered me, her colours, her warmth, an abundance that made everything suddenly too little, starting with the room.

"How about going out?"

"Already?"

We dressed haphazardly, all that mattered was the night in which we would take refuge in the interest of prudence and happiness. I was suddenly content with life, I put all my trust in it, and I immediately accepted, separately and together, the good and the bad it would deem to send me.

We had to go back through the big hall, where Sputter-Jaws and the thin girl with the legs still lingered in a state of perfectly improper abandon.

The darkness welcomed us like two timid birds and wrapped us in its veil. Since it had been raining for the past two days, the river had gone back on its decision and was lapping very close by. There's nothing like lapping water to make a scene complete and a person perfectly happy. Which we were.

"I'll remember you," I stammered with my mouth in her curls. "Whatever happens, I'll remember."

And because it was too much or not enough, because it's our nature to repeat things, we can't do otherwise, we went back through the big hall, saw the decadent couple again, climbed the stairs again, and threw ourselves back on the bed again like dead seaweed on a shore ablaze.

After, a long time after, we came around. Lying side by side, we assessed our inequalities. Our feet were neck and neck, but her knees began long before mine, her thighs stopped their headlong rush in the middle of mine, and our pubes no longer coincided.

Then, words made a reappearance. Question period. All those questions we ask because the bridge needs words to take the plunge into the water.

"Are you married?"

I answered, "No," which was a rather disconcerting response. "It's a waste of time," I explained. "A lot of energy expended for nothing. Not to mention that in nine out of ten cases, statistics say, it all has to be undone and redone. I don't want to be any clearer. Let's just say it's preferable to make your way alone. And when I think that some give it two or three more tries, I'm full of sympathy for them."

"That's my case," said the lady soberly.

"Well, I'm full of sympathy for you."

"You would be even more full if you knew who I'm married to." There was something vaguely triumphant in her tone.

"Do I know him?"

"A little."

We looked at each other for a long moment.

"Not … the man seated to my left?"

She burst out laughing, throwing her head back.

"My, my! How's that for a coincidence!"

"It's not a coincidence." She became serious again. "I can't stand it that my husband attacks just anybody."

"Just anybody?"

"Well …"

"You mean to say it's less myself as a person that attracted you than the fact that your husband was going after that person … well, me?"

She shrugged in a very soft and very amber way.

Thoughts assailed me again, Clotilde, Zita … "I've scattered myself for nothing."

She made a lovely gesture. With the back of her hand, she stroked my cheek. "No, not for nothing."

"For me, it doesn't matter, but to do that to Clotilde …"

"Clotilde?"

"A woman I love but I'm not in love with."

"Why not break it off, then?"

"That's the question I'm always asking myself." I got up and started to put my clothes on. "And that's not all, there was that episode, my unexpected ardour the other day. I can be uncommonly passionate, I'm sometimes quite active, you know."

She batted her eyelashes.

"Well, since that amazing embrace the other day, a very real and passionate embrace during which I completely forgot Zita — forgot Zita, can you believe that? — well, since that night, I've been thinking it's possible that I impregnated. Two people can't cohabit so intimately and with such enthusiasm without something fishy going on."

She had been waving her hands in front of my nose for quite a while. I deduced from this that she was having problems with my reasoning.

"Who's Zita?"

"Another one. *The* other one, in fact."

"Have you told Clotilde about her?"

"We never broached the question, because of all the priority issues between us."

She stood up in turn and made her way toward me, lifting her feet to avoid creasing the clothes that had fallen on the floor, like a soldier on a reconnaissance mission in a minefield. She stroked my back. "You have to tell her."

"You think so?"

She went into the bathroom to repair the damage. When she came back, her hair was all back in place, her dress hung nicely, and she still had hazel eyes.

There was a knock on the door. I opened it. Sputter-Jaws was standing in front of me, his fist raised to knock a second time.

"Good evening, come on in!"

Seeing him so calm, so silent and solemn, with his mouth closed, made him seem more pleasant and no doubt kept me from being afraid.

He handed me a pink slip of paper folded in two. "A message for you. I said I'd give it to you and at the same time retrieve my wife."

I paused for a moment to find the appropriate attitude to adopt in these circumstances.

"Is that you?" asked the woman, approaching.

He put his arm around her waist and they went out the door together.

Just before turning away forever, she came back to me, squeezed my arm, and whispered, "You have to tell her." Sputter-Jaws was already far away, walking with his lowered head bobbing, his hands hanging inert from the sleeves of his rumpled jacket.

～

The message was from Clotilde. I called in spite of the late hour.

"Two pieces of bad news. Which one do I start with?"

"With the worse one."

"That's just it. I don't know which is worse."

"What's going on, Clotilde?"

"Mrs. Le Chevalier has died."

That meant Mrs. Le Chevalier had caught fire. It was hard to imagine any other death for her, and it was exactly what I had feared. Past a certain age, you can't leave them alone for two minutes, you turn your back on them for a second, they go up in flames, old people are like that. Of all the tenants, Mrs. Le Chevalier was the first to go. I felt no shock. How can you be surprised at the death of a woman 110 years old? But someone was gone, someone had left us, and no one, I'd have bet, absolutely no one had asked her where she was going.

"Hermann? Are you there, Hermann?"

"I'm here."

"Okay. Should I continue?"

"Not right away."

I went to the bathroom to throw some water on my face

and look at myself in the mirror. "Goodbye, Mrs. Le Chevalier, goodbye. I'm sorry I wasn't there. But you shouldn't have. Past a certain point, the gods forget us. Especially since your ten elastic years hadn't run out yet. I'll be there tonight and the other nights. For you, I will maintain the deepest silence and I will refrain from all nocturnal activity, in case your voice does me the honour of making itself heard in the dark, talking to me in secret."

"And the other news?"

"Théo's gone."

This news was also foreseeable. Since the beginning, since Clotilde and her moving in with me. Sully had adapted better than Théo, who had preferred to leave.

"How long ago?"

"The day you left, he didn't come home."

"Leave some food on the balcony. And water. Maybe he'll come back."

"Hermann …"

I hung up and went back out into the night. The landscape was the same as before, nature was the same, the river was the same, but nothing was the same anymore. The drunkenness that had taken hold of my limbs to the point of making me feel light and carefree was a thing of the past. An old person had disappeared from the face of the earth, a cat had gone missing. What was so tragic in that? Nothing. So where did this shortness of breath come from, this heart beating out of time, this blurred vision that distorted the stars above my head so that their points, which exist only in children's books, fused together in a blinding mass?

I lay down on the ground, on the carpet of grass that still held the humidity of recent days. Did I blame Clotilde for Théo running away? Of course I did. Would I have blamed Théo if he had made Clotilde run away? My heart started doing it again, a big thump followed by two little ones. It is not necessary to love. It is above all illusory to hope to love all the time. Once you cast a long benevolent gaze on terrestrial creatures, people, plants, animals, once you wish the best for them and for yourself, it is not essential that this love be focused on one of them.

Sleep surprised me in the exact position in which I had lain down, arms in a cross, legs open. Vitruvian Man, pulled in all directions. Not frozen in the perfection of his outstretched limbs, but broken, chaotic, momentarily forgetful of the past and the future, and entrusting his aching body to the earth for a time. Da Vinci might have appreciated it. Maybe he would have bent over me with his contained smile and his broad face, maybe he would have traced a perfect circle, the symbol of the totality of the known universe, around the top of my head to the ends of my hands and my feet using the tip of his index finger. And placed a warm, soothing hand on my belly, where the extreme heat of the body is concentrated, right in the middle of me, right in the middle of the world. At dawn, I felt someone shaking my shoulder. I leapt to my feet, embarrassed, numb. My clothes were damp, dirty, crumpled, and blades of grass and clumps of black earth were stuck to my pants.

The innkeeper was studying me uncomprehendingly. "Do you hate our rooms that much?"

I was determined not to open my mouth; words fail me in the morning.

He opted for laughter. "Come inside, I'll make you some coffee."

I sat down and in silence drank a coffee that was acrid and without much body, but hot, practically boiling. My elbows on the table, I held the steaming cup in front of my mouth and nose to warm them. My eyes were level with the edge of the cup.

The innkeeper walked back and forth in the big kitchen that guests never entered. On the floor near the door I had come in through, there were two stainless steel bowls, one containing water, the other, fish scraps.

"You have a cat?"

"Not back yet," replied the innkeeper. "Maybe you met it last night," he added with a little smile. "It's a night owl, like you."

Then I remembered. In the depths of my unconsciousness,

I had sensed something. A treading in place on my belly, a few movements, then a settling in, a compact warmth. All friends of cats know what I'm talking about, that search for the ideal spot, that circular pawing by the animal that takes up residence on you and borrows you for a while. Its presence hadn't awakened me, it hadn't bothered me either; it had perhaps warmed me, much better than Leonardo's hand.

I made the coffee last until the cat decided to grace us with its presence. As it passed, the flap of the cat door closed with a sharp bang.

It was an animal of respectable size, a male, judging by the width of its head. Its fur was completely grey, except for the paws, which were an immaculate white. Its eyes, jade green ringed with yellow, settled on me, its back arched under my stroking. The next instant, it headed, undulating and graceful, to its morning meal.

26

I arrived home with a serious guilty conscience on my hands, half a dozen cans of deluxe cat food, and an entire flower bed: crimson roses, big speckled irises, gypsophilas, ferns, and so on. It's customary for a person who is unfaithful to make amends.

On the way back, I had made it a point of honour to heap insults on myself: doubly disloyal sham husband, vile libertine incapable of properly sowing his seed, and other more or less damning terms. After which I had taken advantage of a stop of the train to nourish and relieve myself. Even if you harbour a depraved creature within yourself, you have to see to its welfare and feed it properly.

Clotilde was at the stove cooking up something. She had recently gone on a macrobiotic diet, possibly because of my carnivorous cats, who hovered around her whenever she cooked. Despair gripped me, I confess, an ordinary, everyday little despair, the most transient of feelings, but despair all the same – another disembodied meal. Perhaps I should have chosen a restaurant over flowers.

"For you, Clotilde."

I hold it all out to her, cans, flower bed, and guilty conscience, the way you unload a burden. One of the cans falls to the floor and rolls to the door. Sully dashes over, slams it down, and lies on it. Sully without Théo.

Clotilde wipes her hands on her apron and takes the flowers. "Thank you."

The atmosphere is awkward, heavy with embarrassment. The apartment you left three days ago is no longer the same. Something has happened. Clotilde's eyes dart furtively to the dining-room table, where, clearly, they should not be darting. The source of the embarrassment is there.

I look too. A second bouquet of flowers, just about as ostentatious as mine, is sitting right in the middle of the table, high and dry on a lace doily "so it won't make a ring on the wood." In the bouquet, a tiny card presents its blank white side the way a child hides a present behind its back. Clotilde is smiling, but there's still that awkwardness. I turn the card over, there's just one sentence followed by a simple *Clo*, a sentence that sums up what she thinks of me, and what she thinks of me is quite lovely.

I say thank you in turn, I'm completely surprised and flustered.

Why the bouquet? With regard to mine, it's very simple, but hers? Whichever way I look at the question, every answer is more disturbing than the next. Clotilde is giving me flowers because she feels responsible for Théo's leaving or because she too has had her old inn, her river, and her hazel eyes.

I immediately deduce that our relationship is in crisis.

Later, lying in the dark beside her, I will welcome with a relief that's hard to describe as anything other than cowardice the thought that there's reason to hope Clotilde really *does* have someone in her life, so that Zita could tumble into mine without my having to make a choice or lift the least little finger.

～

Alfred had taken care of Mrs. Le Chevalier. I really wouldn't have been able to face her body. Because of our daily encounters, which in fact amounted to very little, because of all those *hellos* and *good evenings* exchanged day after day, I didn't feel I had the right to that relationship. The bodies of old people are hardly bodies. They're usually so fleshless, so empty, nothing is in its place anymore, the skin is barely holding on to the bones, the legs no longer have mass, the fat has melted, they're all spaces, hollows, transparency. Their fingers are claws; their feet, two limp rags. All you want to do is to open your arms and reassemble that tangle of atrophied limbs and sharp angles and hold them tight to you as you hold a fledging fallen from the nest, as you calm the crazed beating of its heart by murmuring words it has never heard.

Old people have that fabulous elegance that permits them to overlook our shortcomings. They see nothing or so little, barely hear anymore, so they confuse things. Or they pretend to be full of indulgence and consideration for our incompleteness. No one exploited Mrs. Le Chevalier's indulgence more than I, pretending sometimes not to see her when I didn't have the heart for it, walking faster in order to get away more quickly. No one took advantage of her absences, her slowness, and her confusion more than I.

27

In less than a week, our two revolutions, Clotilde's and mine, had completely changed the rules of the game. If our previous relations could have been called opaque for the lack of basic spontaneity between two cohabiting individuals, I can say without fear of error that from that moment on, they became downright murky. We avoided each other, to say the least, and I began to lack oxygen, not to mention the fact that the cushion was requisitioned too frequently and threatened with premature wear and tear.

"It's swollen, Mom."

"That's normal when you get older, Hermann."

"I'm not talking about that swelling."

"Oh!" She thought for a few moments. "That's impossible."

"Are you sure?"

"Absolutely. Your father already explained it to you, it seems to me."

"It was kind of vague." I heard her sigh. "You suffer from … secretory azoospermia, the worst kind of all," she added, as if she were laying the cards on the table.

"As far as I know, there are only two types of azoospermia."

"The secretory is the worse one."

"But not necessarily irreversible. Some particularly combative rabbits that have been injected with high doses of testicular spermatids …"

"Hermann, you're neither a rabbit nor particularly combative." She was probably afraid she'd gone too far, because she added more softly, "You can't have children, Hermann. Your father was categorical."

"My father was always categorical. Which didn't stop him from making huge mistakes on many occasions."

She must have been shaking her head sadly. "I'm sorry, Hermann."

"Sorry for what, exactly? Because I can't have children or because they're being made for me elsewhere?"

She coughed. "A little of both."

There wasn't much else to say.

"Tell me about Angela."

"Zita."

"Is she pretty?"

"Not especially."

"That's at least one thing settled. And what does Zita do?"

"The same thing I do. Well, I think so."

"You're made for each other, then."

"If I see her, yes."

"When you see her, you mean?"

"You're amazing, Mom."

"And what about Clotilde?"

"She hardly speaks to me anymore. If she's expecting a child that can't be mine but is pretending to be, it's a case of mistaken identity."

"Maybe you would love that child."

"I love it already, that's the problem."

"You love everything that doesn't exist."

"What no longer exists or does not yet exist, do you understand?"

"I'll try, I promise."

I stood up to wash Mrs. Clémence. I had christened her Valkyrie because of her mouth, her prominent cheekbones, and her shoulders that all looked very Teutonic divinity. The woman was still young, forty, forty-five. She had nice arms and legs. I like it when the arms and legs are divided into clearly defined sections, each separated from the next by a visible joint. Here's the thigh, there's the calf, a thousand miles from each other.

She was equipped to live a hundred years. I continued to wash, my eyes riveted on the mouth that looked so alive. Suddenly, my hand stopped. After all this time, my fingers recognize everything or almost everything. Beside the navel, there was a hole. I went over it a second, then a third time. Where she should only have had a smooth area, there was a break in the flesh. A fissure four or five centimetres wide. When I pressed the edges of the wound, a yellowish liquid came out. I continued to explore the belly, looking for another hole. Usually, knives commit a second offence, they are rarely satisfied with a single cut.

The belly was perforated in two places. Two wounds, one minuscule and, a little higher, the other one, the real one, the one that had killed. The murderer had struck twice. Valkyrie was equipped to live a hundred years, but someone had seen fit to unequip her and shorten her days.

28

Théo did not show up on the day of my return or any of the following days. I continued to let Sully in and out without detecting anything other than an increased nervousness in him, a particular way of sitting up whenever there was even a slight noise at the door or the window. On the evenings when I was not at the laboratory, I'd spend several minutes calling Théo, embarrassed by the sound of my voice but unable to contain myself.

"Do you want to look for him together?" suggested Clotilde.

With my usual intuition, I immediately flushed out the real proposal under the false one. In my mind, I simultaneously translated "Do you want to look for him together?" as "Hermann, I have something to tell you."

And Clotilde indeed said, "Hu came."

"Again?"

"He comes often."

"Right, for the manuscript."

"Not only ..."

Not only?

That was when everything changed. Because even if there was a cat in the bag, with everything happening around me – stiffs, phantom interns, chronic uncertainties, and so on and so forth – an answer like Clotilde's deserved attention.

"Don't tell me ..." I stammered, because I wasn't quite able to make all the connections.

"In the beginning, it was for the manuscript, later ..."

"Don't tell me ..."

"I am telling you, Hermann."

"He's at least 130 years old."

"Eighty-nine. Barely."

"He can't be the father of that child."

"Of those children."

"Oh! How many are there, if I may ask?"

"At last count, there were two."

A small part of the universe cracked.

"You don't produce two kids at over eighty-nine!"

"That's what I thought too."

I didn't need to turn to her to see her smile. Mrs. Claire passed quickly before me. Clotilde had let Hu in and that shrunken old man of eighty-nine had succeeded in forging life, which I had never been able to do. Was that funny? Was it sad? Was everything okay this way or should I immediately roll on the floor screaming?

"Do you think I should feel offended?"

"As you wish," Clotilde replied. "If I were you, I'd feel relieved."

I understood at that moment why Clotilde had come into my life. Her way, in the midst of a crisis, of choosing the practical course. In wartime, Clotilde would work wonders. Dashing from one injured person to another, bandaging wounds, holding a leg in place deaf to the screams of the soldier from whom it was being amputated, Clotilde would have done that, she had that power to neutralize cushions of all kinds. I had an anxious thought for the offspring who would be the objects of such ferocious self-control.

"What nerve! Asking me to read his autobiography!"

"It happened after. Haven't you noticed that he's been avoiding you for a while?"

"How would I have? I've been avoiding him, too."

The irony of the situation did not escape me: Hu's trace, which I had been seeking for so long, was in Clotilde's belly.

29

When I raised my head, Zita was looking at me and smiling. Since the conference, since Clotilde and her brats, she had been more and more present, and I was grateful to her because of Théo.

I took Sigismond out of the cold room and we proceeded with the first washing, side by side, conversing in low voices in case Simone arrived early. Then I opened the laboratory window wide to let in the air and everything it carried. We washed our hands for a long time in silence in front of the mirror over the big sink, our eyes meeting. The time had come, we had to start somewhere, and that somewhere was here, now. We lay down on the floor and exchanged all kinds of warm things, with feelings.

Later, I got up to close the window. I must have been naked, one always is on major occasions. Zita's hand kept watch on my shoulder, Zita on my neck, her waist lingering against my hip.

~

At Simone's arrival, I awake with a start. Since Théo's departure, because of my nocturnal explorations, I've been sleeping badly, I doze off anywhere any time except at night, except in my bed. I hadn't yet finished with Sigismond, I had stopped temporarily as I always do and, as I always do, I was reading.

I greet Simone, and in return I receive all the warmth she's capable of ("I have to clean the labs"), and I'm just thinking that we have been getting along well for at least a week when I see him. Or think I see him. A glimpse of white and black flashing past. I had gone over to the window to observe the night and the city with its lights. There was something hovering in the room. I am completely receptive to illusion and that must be why I see that little white and black meteor that passed the window as my missing cat. A flash. White and black.

I dash off, abandon Sigismond there on his loathsome table, and race toward life outside. I run up and down the streets calling Théo. Every embalmer worthy of the name follows two commandments: silence and the obligation to strive for perfection. Morticians don't talk about what they do, and they do it with impeccable skill. But that's mainly true for the ordinary mortician who works days and hasn't lost a cat.

So I run, I run screaming. I'm disturbing, I know. Théo would already have come to me if he had been that bolt of lightning seen in a moment of confusion. I'm already imagining the neighbours leaving their deep sofas, regretfully abandoning TV sets, the news, it's late-night news time, to pull back their curtains, wondering what nutcase has come to disturb their rest like this. Living close to a funeral parlour isn't all peace and quiet as is mistakenly believed.

I stop, turn around completely, nothing and no one in sight. No cats, no bums. If I looked back, I would see the luminous rectangle that is the door of my laboratory, where Sigismond lies unfinished. I resume my headlong rush, it's like a fight to the finish between me and … and what, in fact? Between me and the absurdity of pointless disappearances.

My steps take me straight to the port. Its smell comes to me, laden with petroleum fumes. I'm always hesitant to go to ports because of all the people with the irrepressible urge to throw themselves in the water. I have no desire to face them.

And it never fails, there is indeed someone. At the end of one of the two piers, there's a man with his back turned, standing stiff as a post, ready to throw himself in. Judging by appearances, he's tall and broad, I would say grandiloquent if he had opened his mouth, which is far from the case, since all I hear, aside from my buzzing temples, is the lapping of the water, which reminds me, just for an instant, of the old inn, the almond woman, and the copper skin.

The man hasn't heard me coming, nothing has moved, not even the folds of the long black cape that covers him from top to bottom. Yet it's hot out, it's summer, but no, he's completely covered, he has that fabulous elegance of a person dressed from head to toe.

"Pardon me, sir, you wouldn't happen to have seen my cat go by?"

I like this opening. It's as if I were saying: "I'll only bother you for a moment, sir. Your fate is of absolutely no interest to me and if you tell me you didn't see anything go by, which would be normal since you have clearly turned your back on true reality, I'll continue on my way and leave you to throw yourself in the water in peace."

So I ask my question about Théo, although I'm already no longer thinking about him, but about the man in black who has his back to me and remains unmoving. I, Hermann, mortician, have just abandoned a dead body to save a future voluntary drowning victim. I've arrived before the fateful fall, guided by a cat that probably doesn't exist anymore and by my formidable intuition, which has led me to Hu.

"Sir?"

Even from the back, he looks sad. Heavy as he is, he would sink like a stone and that's just the opposite of what is needed; you have to be for lightness in all its forms, because the lighter one is, the more chance there is of rising; it's physical.

The man turns around.

"You?" He gives a smile of recognition and then seems about to move toward me, and then nothing.

I say, "If you were counting on doing away with yourself tonight, you've failed."

"How so? Is that what you've come to do too?"

"Not at all. I'm looking for a cat."

In his left hand, a cigarette is burning down, the incandescent tip glowing against the black background.

"Unless my footsteps have intentionally guided me to you, which wouldn't be so surprising, you know how footsteps are."

He doesn't object, doesn't protest. "You didn't come back to see me," he says.

"Why would I have? You know nothing about your father. And as far as I know, we didn't have an appointment."

"No."

"And to be frank, I find you a bit heavy."

He opens the folds of his cape and contemplates himself from feet to plexus.

"I wasn't talking about that heaviness, I was talking about the other kind, the psychological one."

"I see."

"Don't take it the wrong way."

"I'm glad to see you again."

"Me too."

He throws away his cigarette butt and comes toward me. "I don't want to trouble you," he says.

"I was away, out of town. A meeting of people in the trade. I don't like talking about those things."

"Why?"

"One has the right not to like one's trade."

"But you do like it, that's clear. What happened?"

"There was this woman. She had something about her that makes you believe in goodness." I stop talking.

He comes even closer. "You met a woman? Tell me about it."

I take a step back. "I don't feel like it!"

"Oh!" He lowers his head and lights another cigarette. "Don't be angry with me." His movements are awkward, his hands tremble.

"What can I do for you?" I ask.

"Stay here."

"I can't. Not with a laboratory open to the four winds and Sigismond unfinished."

"Sigismond," repeats Hu, separating each syllable.

"He came to me irremediably dead. Like all the others. My life is perhaps a bit lacking in the unexpected."

"If I understand correctly, you shouldn't be here."

"Nor you either."

"I don't have any work left abandoned."

"What would you know about it?"

"Let's walk!"

He leaves me there and goes on his way without turning around. The folds of the cape dance around him. I rush to follow him. I have no idea what I should do. I match my pace to his, giving a thought to the Icebox, the well-lit vestibule that smells of floor polish, and, farther on, to the right, a room that's not much better, my lair, the place of my life. In the cold room, bodies are waiting for me to attend to them. Nothing is really locked. It's not supposed to be. I walk, an outlaw from birth. I walk because he's walking. I never do anything big alone, but if there's someone with me, I can. In front of us there are lighted cafés, and we head inevitably toward the other people.

Hu finally stops, leans against a wall, and stands there looking at the moon. It's round and very beautiful tonight. The seas are visible, mauve against the white crust. I too lean my back against the wall, my shoulder touching his.

"Some people pay tribute to the moon every month by making a wish."

He says nothing.

"Did you know that?"

Around us, people are coming and going, leaving the cafés and movie theatres. They walk around us, look at us, we're partly blocking their way, we are there. A bum comes along, reeling, leans against Hu, who moves slightly. "A thousand pardons, sir, I was passing by, I'm just passing by." His head bobbles as much as he does, his blurry eyes roll and fall on the long cape. An admiring whistle. "Aren't you elegant, my Prince." He moves on, starts reeling again, missing one step out of two – "Uh-oh!" – and plunges into a bar.

I don't know what to say, I'm at a loss for words, even familiar words. Where have the metaphors gone? Yet it's the opportunity of my lifetime. A live one. Just before he cuts the thread. "Don't you find your work depressing?"

I spot a bench, I'm tired. Hu sits down, docile. Close to us, beneath us, I should say, insects are moving around. I hear them. It's actually a bit disturbing because whatever you do, wherever you are, you always hurt something.

"I'm hungry," Hu says suddenly.

I run to the café. I order two sandwiches, two beers. Hu is shivering in spite of the heat. I take off my smock and put it over his shoulders. We eat in order to endure a little longer. The bread is crusty, the ham fresh. Hu shivers even more.

I get up to go for coffee. "You stay here."

He nods slowly as if I've won the first round.

I come back with the coffees. He takes one, puts it down on the bench, lights a cigarette. The little flame wavers and goes out. Hu slips the lighter back in his pocket. The sound of silk.

"Are you married?" he asks.

"Not in the least."

"So ... that woman you met ... what's the problem?"

I sigh. "Life isn't so simple, you know."

"Explain it to me."

In the dim light, his black eyes stare intently at me. I drink my coffee, his remains untouched.

"Clotilde and Zita are two women in my life. Clotilde lives at my place most of the time. Zita persists in staying in my head, which is exhausting. I love them both."

"And the one you met?"

"A third one."

He looks at me, baffled, pulls the folds of his cape around him.

"And you, are you married?"

"Not yet."

"What's her name?"

"Yseult."

He raises both hands, turns them over in the light of the street lamp. I think of Sputter-Jaws, the diamond, and the cut finger.

"What's the matter?" asks Hu.

"Nothing."

He puts a finger on my temple. "What is it?" he insists.

"Horrors."

"Tell me."

And I tell him.

Against all expectations, he laughs, a kind of silent belch that shocks me.

"I don't find it funny!"

"She was dead," says Hu. "And it was only a finger."

"I'm obsessed with integrity."

I try to breathe through my nose, but my body is way too full of air. Hu sips his coffee in silence.

"The other day I had a handicapped man. Do you know what he asked me?"

"No idea."

"He asked me if, when he died, I would also embalm his artificial limbs. The question seems innocuous, of course, but it isn't."

"And?"

"Well, he wanted to know if I was going to preserve his integrity. Were they going to bury everything or only the living part ... well, the non-artificial part. He was seriously incomplete, you know."

"Don't tell me what was missing, I couldn't take it."

"He said that, since he was missing a lot of parts – those are his words, not mine – his soul was probably concentrated in the parts that remained."

I meet only an empty gaze.

"And what did you answer?"

"That I would take the whole thing into account. It all formed a whole. His integrity was both the natural and the artificial, nothing less."

I let a second or two pass.

"I don't have a car anymore because of all the insects that get squashed on the windshield. They leave long streaks, a large part of their organism is reduced to mush, but something continues to fly, what is that exactly, tell me?"

He lights another cigarette. "You're crazy."

"That's not certain."

"Nothing, it's no longer anything at all."

It's suddenly silent, with that particular heaviness that comes from the extreme concentration of molecules. I find it surprising that on this tiny parcel of land on this summer evening, everything that makes human beings noble should be found in such high concentration, that an anonymous bench should be the arena of such formidable tension, two people united by fear, anxiety, hope. Elsewhere, so many people are languishing in front of their TVs, not knowing what to do with their time.

"Have you read Mark Twain?"

"No."

"In his story 'Aurelia's Unfortunate Young Man,' Aurelia has promised a young man that she'll marry him. But, who knows why, the young man in question, his name is Williamson Breckinridge Caruthers, keeps losing pieces. One day, it's a leg he loses in the war, another day, an arm, then he gets sick, he has smallpox, later he's scalped by Indians ... Aurelia remains stoic, but little by little loses her nerve and wonders if she must resign herself to marrying what is left ... You're not listening to me."

"No."

"I wonder about the limit. Beyond what limit is integrity compromised? At what point does a person no longer exist? When half of the person is gone? Three-quarters?"

"I've never asked myself that question."

"Of course you have. Otherwise you wouldn't be here. Because integrity is also talent. And your talent is your hands, but not solely."

He doesn't flinch.

"What's happening to your hands? No, don't hide them!"

I take them in mine and I look at them, as I had done with Alfred. Hu resists for a moment, then lets himself fall against me. His hands are burning, thick, rough, the misaligned fingers have lost their refuge.

"Do you think the talent is still there?" he jokes.

"I think it's in your whole person."

"But if they amputated a foot, I wouldn't lose any of that talent."

"You'd have to see."

"But if they amputated one of these big paddles," he says, raising his hands again. "Or just one of these ten fingers …"

And without warning, he stands up. I do the same.

"You can't stay away any longer," he says as if recess were over. "You have a job to finish."

30

Approaching the lab, I saw Simone outside in front of the door, her wings spread wide like a giant dipteran forced to make an emergency landing.

"Good God, what a welcome!" Hu said ironically.

"Usually she's the soul of discretion. I don't know what's going on."

"The door of a funeral parlour left open, a corpse left – how did you put it? – unfinished, and you're wondering what's going on?"

Our arrival did nothing to calm the overexcited Simone, who would obviously have preferred to see someone other than me.

"HE'S MOVING!" she screamed. "HE MOVED!"

"Calm down, Simone, please. That only happened once. Let's not make a habit of it."

Hu undulated over to her, opened his fabulous cape, and laid a reassuring hand on her shoulder. Beside him, Simone looked more like Simone than ever, social differences had gone out the window.

"Is there the remotest chance, madam, that you might possibly have seen his cat?"

"Well of course I saw his cat! It's on the windowsill! And if you want my opinion, it's not about to go anywhere!"

She pointed a chin toward my person. "He embalmed the thing. He turned it into a mummy!"

"So you embalm cats too?" asked Hu.

"Only on special occasions. Let's go in now."

Simone froze. I went over to her.

"There's nobody moving in there. Come."

"But …" she protested, her index finger pointing at Hu.

"Germs, yes. I'll do what needs to be done."

Hu was already inside, leaning over the table where Sigismond lay. "Is *that* what you do to them?"

That? The disapproval was palpable, and insulting. Yet Sigismond was a complete success. The makeup was perfect, I had preserved the stiffness of his features, which I don't always manage to do, and his colour, which was good.

"That's my work, sir. My work of art. I don't judge your music."

He already regretted his blunder, but the harm was done. I joined him, forced him to bend closer to Sigismond. "Look at him, take a good look. Everything he was is still there. His eyes are half-open because this man never raised them to look at the sky or contemplate a tree. He never really closed them either, which would probably have completely changed the course of his existence. He spent most of his life close to the ground. I feel sorry for him, but that's the way it is. His mouth is naturally closed, I didn't need to sew it, this man has never shouted."

"Sorry. Was he a relative?"

"Not at all."

"How do you know all that?"

"I take what is given me, I imagine the rest."

There was a long silence.

"You said that you didn't judge my music. Well, I'd actually like you to do just that."

"I think we should let it drop," I said. "I have things to do now. I was just leaving."

"He says that," interrupted Simone, "but he doesn't leave, he stays."

"Just to finish Sigismond."

"You could take your revenge," Hu insisted.

"I'm not a critic or a musician."

"I don't need an informed opinion. I want the perspective of a non-expert, of someone who has no musical culture as such, no particular musical sensibility."

"Oh, just anybody's opinion!"

Hu shuddered, as if the words had offended him. "Not just

anybody. I want the opinion of someone with no prejudices, of ... someone pure." He paused. "I want to know if my music can move, can touch the heart of a person like you."

"Why not use me for what I really am?"

"What are you really? I bet you have only the slightest inkling." A pause. "You go to the park with old people every day, you give your opinion on paintings and manuscripts, you run after cats, every day you prepare corpses to prevent them from rotting, and you refuse me the small favour of simply giving me your preference between ..."

"Ask somebody else. You must have acquaintances, friends."

"Flatterers, liars incapable of telling me what my faults are, whether my interpretations are successful or unsuccessful, whether I'm progressing or regressing. And even they are gone," he added. Another pause. "Do me this one small favour and ... I promise you I won't go back to the port. Except to see Yseult, of course."

"Yseult lives at the port?"

"Very nearby. We don't live together," he added.

"And that suits her? She doesn't insist that you do? Clotilde would like us to live together officially. She likes things that are official."

Simone raised her eyes to heaven and disappeared without further ado, accompanied by her pails.

"And you don't want to live with her?"

I shrugged..

"Because of Zita?"

"Something like that."

I covered Sigismond again and started to tidy up.

"I'd like to share a meal with you," Hu proposed.

"I can't."

"In that case, let's go see Zita."

I stiffened, panic-stricken.

"Why not?" he protested. "It seems she's the most important person in your life, and you haven't talked to her yet. And what about Clotilde? What are you waiting for to make a decision?"

I didn't have an answer, I was much too busy trying to swallow. My heart was pounding against my ribs and I was in pain. Everything suddenly seemed pointless to me, pitiful. I was still wearing the smock I had worn this morning; it was grey, dirty, much too short. My gloves were old, the mask too, my shoes were no longer waterproof; in my right hand, which was trembling, the trocar gleamed feebly. Some people have the gift of an aura of light they take with them wherever they go. Woe to those who remain in the shadows.

"Maybe we shouldn't try to keep everything, to preserve everything," murmured Hu. "Maybe you have to choose. To let go. Among the thousand and one possibilities life offers us, to choose one and use it up, exhaust it. Until there's nothing left of it." He was trembling like a willow in the wind. "You never have the time, anyway. You can't do everything."

"What are you talking about?"

He grabbed my arm. "That's what I've done. I didn't try anything at all, I concentrated on one thing, I missed out on everything else, but maybe I was right, what do you think? You can't be somebody else, you don't choose what you are."

I shook myself free. "You're the crazy one now!

He gave a start and moved away. "Please don't be angry with me."

"I'm not angry with you."

"We're going to eat together, that's the appropriate thing to do now."

"I have to leave, Simone is waiting for us to leave."

"I've never been with a woman, you know." He looked stricken, as if the revelation had come from me and not from him. He waited for me to react, to say something.

"What about Yseult?" I finally managed to ask.

He shook his head slowly without taking his eyes off me. "Never. Not a single one."

I tried not to let anything show, but I moved, I think. Because of the strangeness of the scene. I said nothing while the broad outlines of a universe, his universe, took form in my mind.

The telephone rang. I picked up the receiver. Clotilde.

"I'll be home soon," I said. "I'm closing up and coming home."

Is it because of Hu, because of that confession made in the middle of a laboratory stinking of death and disinfectant, that it seemed urgent that I go home to be near Clotilde?

"I'm coming home, Clotilde."

But Hu grabbed the receiver. "Is that the famous Clotilde? If you only knew how happy I am to make your acquaintance, madam." He bowed to her. In front of me, his only audience, out of courtesy to a woman who didn't even see him.

"We were going to go out for a bite, Clotilde. Come with us ... Who am I? A friend. Come, please. No, it's not late. Come. We're going to eat together and then ... we'll go see Zita."

I just had time to clear off the chair and collapse into it.

31

Everything was absurd. Clotilde sitting at the table in the café between Hu Junior and me. The same café, Clotilde's, which in a way is also mine. Hu was recounting I don't know what, and Clotilde was listening. He had a talent for talking, she had a propensity for listening, as soon as she was the object of undivided attention and Hu's gaze enveloped her and concentrated her into a single sensitive, vital point. She was leaning toward him in that attitude of the body bending toward another, distracted for a while from all cares, all self-interest, all weight. Hu spoke and everything became strangely simple, plausible. My relationship with Clotilde, so constrained, so unnatural. I looked at her, perhaps for the first time. Nothing was settled, no, but there was a moment when I saw from far away, outside myself, these two people, so close and so distant, who had not known each other a minute before but who had in common that they shared a part of my life. Afterward, nothing would have changed. Clotilde would still be Clotilde, and Hu would still be Hu, a person dedicated to a single cause, who had already begun to disintegrate and for whom I could do nothing. For the time being, I saw only his lips that were moving and his eyes that penetrated the depths of Clotilde. How had someone so physical, so visibly enamoured of other people, been able to do without them for so long? Looking at him, you had the impression of a pent-up torrent that suddenly bursts its barriers and pours out.

Some disasters are pure masterpieces. Two people converse in friendship and respect, they're sitting there in a simple café under ordinary lighting, they're talking, and the world finally stops its racket. That's what we're here for, that and nothing else, if only it would last, if only it would never stop.

~

"At the next light, turn left," said Hu. "It'll be the next one on the right."

Zita lived at the other end of town. Hu had wormed the address out of me and had insisted on paying for the taxi, raising his index finger, pointing left, right, and left again like an orchestra conductor beating time. I was looking at my knees, anywhere but outside, anywhere but at Clotilde, anywhere but at the streets streaming by, cutting down my meagre defences and the distance separating me and Zita.

My dream was almost a year old, some last a lifetime. The taxi braked one last time, I was thrown forward.

"Here we are."

What followed is still vague in my memory. It had much too much to do, it didn't register my getting out of the taxi and stretching my numb limbs or Clotilde's confusion at being unceremoniously dropped into my secret garden or Hu's easy way of slamming the door and leaning toward the window to pay.

But it remembers the three of us in front of Zita's window, our eyes raised toward an absurd and uncertain future. The building was rundown, covered with beige bricks, some of them loose, and it was six storeys high. It was late, the windows were dark. Maybe she's already gone to bed, I thought. Maybe she's asleep, her fists clenched; that's it, she's asleep, we won't see anything, no sheer curtain, no silhouettes, no suggestive shadows kissing like in the movies and shattering the dreams of solitary dreamers.

I had waited so long, hesitated so long, and here I was in front of her door at almost midnight, a timid soul who's put off by the mere prospect of making a phone call in full daylight and who shows up at night with his girlfriend and a bare survivor in front of the apartment of a woman he's been close with only in his thoughts.

I don't know how much time passed. The heat had subsided, but the humidity gave the streets, cars, and street lamps an oily look. The moon had a halo that made it appear bigger.

"We should leave now."

"Not yet," said Hu.

Time passed. There was no point in our waiting.

"What you love is right here," murmured Hu, looking up at the building. "Remarkably concentrated here," he added, putting his arm around Clotilde's shoulders, "in this single point, this building, this apartment. Compared to the universe ... it's really quite extraordinary."

I would have liked to reciprocate, to ask him all the questions I hadn't had time to ask: whether he loved Yseult, why he hadn't known any other women, why his house was a stronghold of solitude that made any presence incongruous, why we had so quickly lost interest in his father ...

"Let's go in," said Hu.

"Absolutely not!"

He pushed the door open and we went into a large entrance hall, with him in front, me in the rear, and Clotilde between us, moving like a sleepwalker. On the left-hand wall, there was a bin piled high with unclaimed newspapers and flyers; on the right, a row of dilapidated mailboxes each with a greyish button worn down by the fingers that had pressed it year after year. Some tenants had written their full names, as if to say, "I live here, hurry up and come see me!" Others had just put two initials, or nothing at all. Zita's name didn't appear anywhere.

Hu came over to me. He took a pair of glasses from his pocket and examined the mailboxes for a long time. "What floor does she live on?"

"The second. I think," I added, glancing at Clotilde.

Hu put the tip of his index finger on one of the grimy little buttons and pressed it. We waited, nothing happened. Clotilde sighed, I would have liked to do the same.

Hu rang again. I gulped air like a fish out of its bowl, grabbed Clotilde's hand and squeezed it.

"I'm sorry," I muttered through clenched teeth. "So sorry."

She was in profile, the left, my favourite one of all, and her lips were trembling.

"When I'm dead," asked Hu, "will you come get me?"

"You won't be dead."

"But when it does happen?"

"Quiet!"

He was suddenly getting on my nerves. This moment was not his but mine. And Clotilde's. Her hand was still in mine, without warmth but without animosity, abandoned there like a thing you give up because you don't really care much for it anymore.

"I'd like you to come to my place," said Hu.

"No."

"Tomorrow."

The door suddenly opened behind us, a current of warm air blew into the entrance hall, and two men entered, a big, solid, long-legged guy of about fifty with a long, bony face, and a younger man wearing jeans with holes at the knees and a black leather jacket.

"Pardon me, sir?" Hu asked the older man. "We're looking for a woman by the name of Zita."

There was a long silence. Clotilde's hand deserted mine. To avoid asphyxiation, I turned around and looked outside.

"Never heard of her," declared the man. "What about you?"

The young man hesitated. "There are twenty-four apartments. I don't know everybody. You didn't see her name?"

And then it happened. The door opened a second time and Zita appeared.

I hardly recognized her, I had been carrying her with me for so long, dreams are never true to life. But it was really her. The bleak light from the ceiling fixture lit only her, that's the way it was, it's chance, but even with no light, I would have seen her. Dreams are never true to life, but they do what they can. My brain went back several months. Zita, her coal-black eyes fixed on me, so attractive in her multipocket jumpsuit with her paraphernalia of tubes and household products, so tall and so broad in my suddenly narrow laboratory. And now, she was here, ten steps away from me, ten steps away from

Clotilde, and she was not alone. At her side, very close to her, a man was telling her something funny; his lips were brushing her ear and she was laughing. The man was Alfred.

Hu didn't see anything, but continued asking questions, or perhaps he was engaged in conversation with the two men. In any case, there was background noise, sentences exchanged, no doubt, while Alfred and Zita looked at the little group we formed, like a plug that kept them from going inside.

"Sorry," said Alfred. "Excuse us."

And Zita still laughing and me backing up, backing up farther, as far as the wall, the one on the right, the one with the buttons, my terrified back pushing roughly against it, setting off buzzers, triggering the mechanism in the door, which was clicking.

For a moment, it was them and me, their six pairs of eyes riveted on my body pinned to the wall, while above our heads the intercom spat out sleepy protests and questions that went unanswered.

"Hermann," murmured Alfred.

Zita's eyes, surprised, Clotilde's eyes, huge under their border of black eyelashes, half-frightened, half-pitying. Alfred took a step toward me, but it was Hu who grabbed me by the shoulders and pulled me toward him to silence the buzzers.

Then? Nothing. I can't go further, I can't imagine what came next. Everyone has their own powers of description, mine are limited, at least with respect to the relationship my person maintains with those who touch it most closely.

I only remember the warmth. That of Clotilde and Hu flanking me as we left — two guards escorting a condemned prisoner — Clotilde's shoulder weighing on my arm, Hu's, higher, lighter. And this painful observation: dreams may not be matter, they must be light to dissolve like this, while the instant before, they were weighing down your heart with all their heaviness.

Hu's voice came to me from far away. "I'm sorry."

I stopped and turned to him. His tall frame hid the street lamp, which gave him a halo. "Me too."

He came close to me and closed his hand, his knuckles tapped softly against my burning forehead. "Let's walk," he said.

⌇

Arm in arm, we walked all night, an endless, silent walk that allowed us to get through the worst. At dawn, we stopped by mutual agreement, exhausted, our limbs heavy, and looked for a place to set down, extraterrestrials newly arrived on an unknown planet. Day was breaking, the first cafés were coming to life, delivery trucks were unloading goods into outstretched arms or onto shiny rails that caught the first rays of the sun. It was going to be a beautiful day, one of the first of this summer that had begun with grey skies and rain. In the houses, people were yawning, stretching endlessly, opening curtains, washing themselves, the plumbing was groaning, ablutions. Around us, too, sounds were waking up, spoons were being put down on saucers, dishes proclaiming their usefulness, the aroma of coffee rising higher and higher. Someone was speaking to a dog. Life was reassembling its atoms, gently getting moving again.

Hu led us to a café. I had no idea where we were. A new neighbourhood where I recognized nothing, not the streets, not the businesses, not the houses. We fell into seats in front of three black coffees and a pile of toast, which Clotilde and I did not touch. Hu consulted us with his eyes before wolfing it all down. He wiped his mouth with a rather precious little gesture.

Sitting across from me, Clotilde, usually so pink, was pale as could be and was shooting me little embarrassed looks from time to time. Under her thin raincoat, her belly was burgeoning. As I had the night before, I looked at her for a long time, with all I had left of courage and affection. Clotilde looked back at me and we exchanged a smile, a beautiful open smile that forced our hands to come out of their lairs to approach each other and join together. Hu looked at us without understanding. With a definitive graceful rippling movement of her rounded shoulders, as if she were shedding her skin and finally allowing herself to be seen, Clotilde freed her arms from the raincoat and grabbed Hu's big hand and placed it on her belly.

"Two children of the winter," she said, smiling.

Hu stared at her, his eyes surprised, his desperate hand having a hard time touching the thin fabric screen that separated it from Clotilde's flesh. So it was true. He had never. Not a single one. How was it possible? How had this gigantic body built to take, to seize, to enjoy, never found an opportunity to join with another body, even if it meant losing itself, even if it meant giving in? As always, because I can't help it, I saw the child, the boy, the tall stature, the low forehead, some would have said stubborn, the thick legs, the endless arms. This strange assemblage had never been offered to any woman. Yet Clotilde was looking at him, she was smiling at him, this big Buddha had something, a certain totally animal something that could make you want to throw yourself on him, lose yourself in him.

"Congratulations!" stammered Hu, looking at me.

He had withdrawn his hand and was squeezing Clotilde's, as he must do all the time, compensating with this ardour focused on an innocuous object for his failure to pursue more compromising flesh.

I smiled. "She's the one who should be congratulated, not me."

Hu looked at us each in turn, unsure how to respond.

"I'm a sterile undertaker. Could you imagine anything lower?"

Hu clapped his hand over his mouth. Clotilde gave a gentle shrug, pouting. I think I laughed. Judging by the surge in my gut, the contractions of my abdomen, and the painful waves the zygomaticus major and minor were causing in my features, I must have smiled. Once the first moment of surprise had passed, Clotilde and Hu looked at each other before joining in the merriment that was gradually spreading among our neighbours, two businessmen hidden behind their newspapers, page one of which actually described the horror of the L'Aquila earthquake, a group of workers sitting at the bar, and a wobbly old gentleman who took advantage of the opportunity to raise his glass, and a certain number more, to our health.

"But then …?" asked Hu, which was the normal question to ask.

"They're your father's."

He grimaced and then nodded. "More of his traces, if I understand correctly." Then, realizing his lack of sensitivity, he stammered, "My father is like that," looking at Clotilde. "In any case, he's very lucky."

The café gradually emptied out. We got up.

Hu turned to me. "See you tonight."

"I don't think so."

"I'll be expecting you."

"I won't come."

"Tonight, eight o'clock."

He pushed us outside, hailed a taxi, opened the door, stepped aside to let us get in, and closed the door.

I rolled down the window. "You aren't coming?"

Hu bent down to the window. "I'm happy to have made your acquaintance."

Then he made a grandiose gesture. He put his hand on my neck at the place where you slaughter an animal, you know, that point on the neck. He straightened up and strode away. The black silk of his shoulders gleamed in the sun.

All the cells must be saturated. Once the abdominal cavity has been emptied, once the gases, the surplus blood, the contents of the stomach, and the urine have been extracted, you have to saturate everything, all the cells, all the tissues. But there are traces. No one sees them, but I do. On my hands, my wrists, a fine grey, rather stubborn film. Sometimes it sticks. No matter how much you scrub, it resists. Sometimes it disappears on its own or melts into my skin. A "necessary evil," Julian and Alfred claim, and they hasten to add that the only way to get by honourably in this profession is to live in formalin, physically and mentally.

I believe I have felt the need to be inhabited by another person more than anybody else has. To experience the flutter of a beating heart that is not your own, the vibrations of another body, the air flowing in and out of the lungs, the warm blood, I believe I need this more than others. Or with greater urgency. The physiological body is the opposite of an abstraction, it is the only certainty we have. We mustn't underestimate the power of this warmth that cuts you off from the night and corrupts your soul. Or its effect. The ineffable miracle.

32

Simone was there, all I saw was her back. Without that back, nothing would have happened. I went over and grabbed her in a bear hug. Women hate that, I know. But I grabbed her, yes. She stiffened a little more, bleach seeped from every pore of her skin.

"Don't move, Simone, please. Just for an instant. Sometimes that's enough."

She froze. She didn't have much choice, I was holding her tight, my profile against hers, my two hands filled with her breasts. If anyone had seen us. Except for the broom handle that was hurting my arm and the awful smell, it could have been a pleasant encounter. Get to the point. In emergencies, forget about the details, even if they're assailing your nose, your mouth, your pounding heart. Sometimes, the person doesn't matter, only the sex counts, the opposite sex, I mean, the one that's not yours and never will be, that mixes its colours, its climates, with yours, that consciousness of what you are not. I have never felt such an immediate, devastating need for the close presence of a stranger's warmth, a sexual warmth.

I must have squeezed too hard, Simone belched. The sound was quite clear, the familiar sound of a corpse yielding.

"I'm sorry, Simone."

She suddenly freed herself and fled to the washroom. The broom fell to the floor with a whip-like snap. My open arms had the exact dimensions of Simone.

"I'm sorry, Simone. Sorry, sorry. There was nothing you could do."

She was vomiting there, I was crying here. I imagined her thin, frail body shaken by spasms. I went to the door.

"Simone? Are you okay, Simone?"

I didn't hear anything. Then the sound of the toilet flushing. Simone was alive, she had survived. She came out all white and stiff, wreathed in a human smell.

"Don't ever do that again!"

⌇

Mrs. de Valois was in the park, I was at her side without being there, dead with fatigue, nauseous, elsewhere, but where? I didn't recognize much on her canvas anymore, but it was as if, now, I didn't care. I thought of Clotilde, of Zita with Alfred, his blue-veined hands on Zita, and I thought of Hu. I thought of the incoherence of dreams and the weight of living beings. I thought of a world with no attachments, would we be lighter, freer?

Mrs. de Valois was totally absorbed in her canvas; she backed up a little, appeared to admire it. She even smiled.

"It's finished," she said.

"Really?"

My surprise didn't offend her, she had the assurance of someone who had produced a work of art.

"How do you know it's finished? What signs do you see that it's finished? How can you show such assurance?"

"I just know," she answered with the same decisive smile as before.

"And you're satisfied with it?"

"Very," she said.

"That's rare, an artist satisfied with a work. Usually, they say there's a huge gap between what they've done and what they tried to do. Usually they say, 'Is that all?' And they're disappointed. A way of indicating that, within, it was much more beautiful, much greater!"

"What's happened to you, my boy? Did you not sleep well?"

"I didn't sleep at all. I lost two people at one time. Clotilde is still there, but they're three now, without my having anything to do with it. I don't know how to act with her anymore, with them rather, and she doesn't either. Even her birds look lost, her gyrfalcon is not at all true to life, it looks like a swan with claws, not to mention Hu Junior, who's going downhill. Everything is messed up, I have to re-examine everything, draw up a balance sheet. Nothing is as I thought it was, I can glimpse what the liabilities may look like, but I have no idea of what I should put under assets."

"Calm down, child. Hu has a son?"

"Of course. And he's a musician. And unlike you ..."

"Not the pianist?"

"In person. Do you know him?"

"Only by reputation. An immense musician."

"Huge, I would say. But unlike you, he's not at all satisfied. He's obsessed with his shortcomings. He considers himself mediocre, in the old sense of *average*, so he's always at the port. If that's not a liability, what is it, I ask you?"

"Good heavens!" exclaimed Mrs. de Valois, as if the solution was to be found there. She abandoned her canvas. "That's awful!"

"And there's nothing I can do to get him out of there. I can't spend my days at the end of the wharf. I already let Mrs. Le Chevalier get away."

"I understand."

"Heels is sick, did you know?"

"No."

"So I take Mrs. Fitzback out for some fresh air. Usually, it's the other way around. It's not easy."

"No, of course not."

"Have you ever seen Mrs. Fitzback without her dog?"

"Never."

"She's unrecognizable. She walks behind me with her head down and stops as soon as I stop. It's rather disconcerting. It's quite a production to get her going again beside me."

"I sympathize completely."

"He promised me he wouldn't go back to the port on condition that I go to his place tonight."

"You'll go, I hope."

"Of course."

"He mustn't be left alone."

"I can't be everywhere."

Mrs. de Valois's gaze fluttered from the pond to the fountain, and from the fountain to the canvas. A habit of many months that had given rise to this jumble of ambiguous shapes, this unidentifiable mutant object. *Wanderings*.

"What do you plan to do with the painting? Put it in a gallery?"

"Never, not for the world," protested Mrs. de Valois.

"What, then?"

She smiled at me. "Give it to you, my boy."

"Give it to me?"

"Why, yes."

"To me?"

"To you."

Where Mrs. de Valois saw the obvious, I saw only misunderstanding. "Why me, exactly?"

"Why, because it's you, my child. That's you, there," she added, pointing her finger at the centre of the pond.

It wasn't possible.

"There's no way that could be me."

"Why not?"

"I'm not a pond."

"Nobody thinks any such thing."

"Even less, dry water or a stationary pedestrian, although ..."

"No, no, of course not."

"I don't see myself like that at all."

"Everyone has their own way of seeing."

"I only look good from the back."

"Who put such an idea in your head?"

So it was me. That circle of false pond, that water, my face, my hair.

"Well, I like you from the front."

She grabbed me by the shoulders and looked straight at me. My face, my hair, that look of recognition. My expression.

When I think that all this time I've been walking around with myself under my arm!

"It's terrible," I said.

"What?"

"Hu saw a bison."

"Don't worry about Hu."

"I cannot in all decency accept being confused with a bison. Even less with a buffalo."

"Hu doesn't understand modern art."

"Or metaphor."

"Or metaphor!"

She started to put away her things. ·

"You'll accept it, at least?"

What a question! How do you answer when someone offers you a double of yourself?

"It's a deal," said Mrs. de Valois. "And all the same, you do like it a little?" she added humbly. "You don't look very happy."

Then I did an extraordinary thing, I walked up to the easel, I grabbed the canvas, as I had Mrs. de Valois earlier, and I took a good look at myself.

"You're pale all of a sudden," said Mrs. de Valois.

"It's not every day you have a chance to meet yourself, is it? But I suppose the experience is worth it."

She was still putting things away, gathering brushes, paints, and rags.

"Is this the end of our meetings?"

She surveyed the park. "I think I'm finally going to paint this park. With all your talk about it, you've managed to convince me."

33

The door was ajar. He was sitting close to the piano in a high-backed armchair that completely hid his head. He stood up when I came in, put a glass in my hand, and asked how my day had been.

"Well, I spent a good part of the morning trying to open my eyes. Then I called SOS Suicide, but they were overloaded. I also contacted Youth Protection, but they said I was too old. That meant I had time to go to the park with an old friend. She gave me this."

I showed him the painting.

"Oh yes," said Hu. "The old lady."

"You know her?"

"Kind of. You're not the only one who goes to parks."

He looked exhausted, his hair was pulled back, he was wearing a white shirt with a black velvet jacket. We sat down facing each other.

I drank. "So? What do you think?"

"It's you, there's no doubt about it. You're recognizable. I recognize your eyes. She had trouble with the eyes, but she finally got them right."

My eyes, those two surprised black buttons topped with two hairy little up-arrows? "How do I manage to miss so many things? I have trouble transposing, you know? I don't have an awful lot of imagination."

"But you have sensitivity."

"Hang on! I have to stop you there."

"I haven't said anything yet."

"But you're going to."

"I'm only asking you for an opinion of my work. I certainly judged yours! I even came close to telling you that what you were doing to your dead bodies was improper. Take your revenge! It's your turn to judge me!"

"You didn't judge anything at all, for the simple reason that you wouldn't be capable of it, I'm the one who told you that Sigismond was a success, you wouldn't have seen anything. You have no idea what I do, and I don't know anything about music."

"So much the better."

"We're strangers to each other and we should stay that way."

"Why so?"

I didn't say anything, because I could see very well that the trap was closing.

"We're not strangers to each other," said Hu. "We've shared meals, I know Clotilde, you led me away from the port. What I'm asking of you isn't much: to give me your opinion on two interpretations … no, three." He stood up. "Unless all you're good for is emptying corpses!" He waited, hoping the insult would have an effect.

"It's been a long time since I've taken offence at such remarks, sir. But it's unworthy of you and of me."

He dropped down onto the piano bench and passed one of his big hands over his face, the left hand, the one that trembled less. I thought back to last night, which had been torn between hope and disappointment, a painful schism that was forcing me to rebuild a future for myself. How can you not hate those who destroy dreams?

I walked over to the window and looked outside. My breath made a fog on the glass.

"Leave now," he said. "That would be best."

But I couldn't. I can't leave a room unless I'm the last one. I went over to him, touched his shoulder.

"Leave me alone!"

So I gave in. For better or for worse. I sat down again without saying a word and I waited for what would come next, my eyes closed.

At first, nothing happened. Then I heard him rummaging

through his record collection. Sounds of buttons being pressed, plastic against plastic, clicks, humming.

He came over to me, leaned on an arm of the chair, his smoky breath in my ear. "I'm going to have you listen to the same piece three times. I don't want to know which interpretation is the best, I only want to know which one you like best."

He walked away, it was going to start. Buttons pressed. The music rose. I listened with all the enthusiasm, all the concentration I was capable of. He paced back and forth in the big dimly lit living room. I listened to the music and the sounds of his presence.

The piece ended and it was silent in the room. Without saying a word, Hu took out the CD and replaced it with another, and I heard pretty much the same music. What was I doing here and what was the point of all this? What use was it to him to know I preferred the first interpretation to the second or the third?

I asked him to let me hear the three interpretations again. He complied without protest. I listened a second time, then a third. And I saw, of course. The first and the third interpretations were very similar, they had a common approach, an identical spirit. The second one stood out from the other two.

"I'd like to hear the first and the third again. Then the second," I said.

I immediately closed my eyes again. I knew it would be over after this. My heart beat violently in my chest and I started to breathe through my mouth.

"What's the matter?" asked Hu.

I motioned to him to be quiet. "Once more."

I listened again. And once again. I knew the piece, I knew what was coming, I could hum it, I saw the differences. I opened my eyes. "You aren't the performer in all three interpretations."

Hu backed away. A slight, frightened movement. "I didn't say all three were mine."

"But you presented them as if they were."

"So?"

"So it's not the case. The first and the third are by the same pianist, the second is by a different one."

"You're free to believe that. And which interpretation do you like best?"

"Why should I tell you?"

"Because I'm asking you."

I shook my head slightly. "No."

"Out of friendship."

"Still no."

He took the blow without wavering. "You have a favourite, I know it."

"Yes."

"But you won't tell me which one."

"No."

He turned away, walked over to the piano, shook his head, and pivoted toward me. "Why hesitate? You have one chance in two of picking my interpretation."

"And what if I was wrong? What if I preferred the other pianist?"

"It's just a game, nothing more. You don't actually think your opinion is that important to me?"

"Of course it is."

He came back over, grabbed my shoulder. "Do it for me, please."

His breath stank. I'll bet he hadn't eaten anything since the morning.

"In return, I'll give you this." He held a big soft package out to me. The brown envelope forgotten at the fruit seller's.

"How long have you had it?!"

His only answer was to shake the package feebly. "You're not the only one who goes to parks, you're not the only one who goes to markets. You shouldn't have forgotten it there," he concluded, with a nasty smile.

The envelope was crumpled but intact. He hadn't even opened it.

"I would have given it to you in the end," he said with a funny intonation in his voice. "Either to you or to the old lady."

"But you didn't."

I turned to leave.

"At least take the envelope," Hu shouted.

"I don't need it anymore. Your father's life doesn't interest me anymore."

"If you leave now, we won't see each other again."

"We won't see each other again anyway."

He ran to me, grabbed me, and shoved me against the wall. "Please. I need to know," he said, pronouncing each word separately. "I'm asking you as a favour." He was breathing hard and his forehead was glistening with sweat. "How can I make you understand?" he whispered. "There's something in you that's out of the ordinary, I don't know how to define it. It's why Clotilde isn't able to leave you, why Mrs. de Valois paints you, why my father entrusted you with … this!" He lowered his eyes and let go of me. "Something that makes it impossible to turn away from you," he finished, embarrassed.

Mrs. de Valois had said, "I like you from the front."

As I was going through the door, I turned around one last time. "All three of them are you, aren't they?"

Silence.

"The first and the third interpretations bear the mark of youth, of spontaneity. There's passion, fervour. The second is more controlled. It must be more recent. You're observing yourself, you're watching yourself, the spirit isn't there anymore, nor the generosity."

Hu stood unmoving, his broad face devoid of emotion.

What I didn't say: in the second interpretation, some notes are heavy, they stick, your fingers can no longer move away in time, they're too thick.

34

I only have a confused memory of the next day. I was bent over a body, ideas and feelings were mixed up in a jumble, with Hu's suffering, Clotilde's, mine, and quite certainly, Alfred's, melted together in a sore spot in the middle of my thorax.

Clotilde went back to her place, which was the best thing to do. Simone had become transparent again, I saw through her, objects, the walls, even the landscape outside. Julian and Alfred came and went behind me, sometimes brushing past me or standing motionless at my door, without my deigning to look up, because I didn't know what to say, and especially, didn't feel like saying it.

Alfred finally made a decision. I felt his presence behind me, that closeness I can't stand when I'm working.

"Someone left this for you, Hermann."

I barely turned. Stuck to the brown envelope was a sheet of paper folded in two.

"On the pile of books," I muttered.

Alfred set the package down carefully. He stayed there, waiting. "Hermann …"

My hand increased its pressure on the body of the young girl. She was eighteen, no breasts, no hips, nothing but bones and an empty stomach.

"Try to understand, Hermann …"

"I do understand, that's the worst thing."

"Since the child died, it's been a desert at home, I can't bring myself to touch her anymore, I can't do it. It's as if she's become a stranger."

"You should have told me."

Silence.

"Julian knew?"

"Not in the beginning. Later, I told him."

"Him and not me!"

"When could I have done it? You work in the evening, in the daytime, we never know if you're here or not. I tried, I really tried. But you're so weird, so absent. And you seemed ..."

At that, I straightened up and faced him.

"Fond of her? Well, yes, why not?"

His voice became hard. "That's no way to love, in a vacuum. You should have made it known!"

"I don't do that kind of thing!"

He turned away, lowering his head. "Oh! Anyway ..."

"Anyway, it wouldn't have done any good, would it? Zita threw herself into your arms? It was you, not me? From the beginning?"

I would really have liked him to protest, no, no, not at all, I'm the one who went after her. I would really have liked there to be that doubt, that hesitation. I would have wanted Zita not to have known right away, but to have felt a benevolent neutrality that gave us each a chance.

Alfred only looked relieved. "She's the one who came to me, she ... she noticed me right away." Then, realizing his cruelty, "That's what she told me, anyway."

He suddenly collapsed onto the envelope and the pile of books. The little tower fell over in a heap of crumpled paper, Alfred with it. He remained seated on the floor, bawling like a calf, his face buried in his two blue hands.

"It was so good, you have no idea, Hermann, you have no idea ..." He shook his head, gasping for air.

Julian rushed over.

"It's as if she had guessed," Alfred hiccupped, "as if, in this world" (he made a vague gesture toward the ceiling) "there was someone watching over me, understanding me, someone on my side. My side."

Julian was observing the scene with a hint of disapproval in his face. "How about getting back to work?"

The note was short, with no signature:

I am returning what belongs to you. Would you do me the honour of visiting me one last time? This evening, eight o'clock.

I crumpled up the sheet of paper and opened the envelope. The work was 259 pages long, the cursory binding contrasted with the elegant typography, which was a bit affected, as was the title: *In Praise of the Small: The Greatness of Miniatures*. It wasn't an autobiography in the usual sense, but rather a kind of hybrid essay combining reflections on art and slices of life, the work of an aesthete who felt it useful to bequeath to posterity the traces of a life dedicated to beauty.

⌇

"How's Sonia?" asked my mother.

"Zita."

"How's Zita?"

"I don't know. She's not here anymore."

"She never was, it seems to me. Was, in the true sense," she took care to specify.

"As you wish."

My mother sighed. My mother likes clear situations. Like Julian and Alfred. "Could you be more precise?"

"She preferred someone else."

Another sigh, I heard her move her chair.

"Am I disturbing you?" I asked.

"Of course you're disturbing me, Hermann. What do you think? That old people have nothing to do? But I'm staying, you see? I'm staying. I'm sitting and I'm staying. To listen to you, only to listen to you. And I'm sighing because I'm tired, that's all. So please, don't take everything so personally, okay?"

"Okay."

"Clotilde is a nice person. If she was placed in your path, maybe there's a reason."

"Yes, but what is it? I'm not able to see my life from above, as a whole. If I could, I'd be able to see Clotilde's place in it. From down here, I can't see anything."

"What happened, Hermann?"

"I don't know."

She didn't say anything, she must have felt useless.

"I love Clotilde for everything she will never get from me, for what I can't give her. To live, to really live, you have to have someone to watch, that's what parents do with children, they watch them and hope they live, do you understand?"

"I understand."

"I'm not sure I watch Clotilde. It's terrible. Because as soon as people no longer have someone to watch them, they die, it's well known."

"Do you want me to come over?"

"No. I only wanted you to know."

I heard her blow her nose.

"Mothers are free, Hermann. When they're old, you should leave them in peace. For the road they still have left to travel."

"I'm sorry."

"What I mean is, you should keep going. Even if you don't see anything."

"I work with dead tissue, Mom."

"Well, show you're worthy of it, Hermann."

"Worthy?"

"The work you do is a worthy occupation. Whether you think so or not."

"You've never said that to me, no one has ever said that to me."

"Your father said it to you hundreds of times, but since it was your father, you didn't hear."

I was stunned. "He spent his whole life hoping people would stay alive, I spend practically all mine waiting for their demise. An embalmer who's a doctor's son is an anomaly."

She let some time pass. I didn't. "Did you love him?"

She hesitated just a fraction of a second. "People's love doesn't concern you."

"Of course it concerns me. It concerns everybody."

"Good gracious, Hermann." She must have been looking around her for a life raft, a Medusa. "Love is not something that is counted. It's not something you use up …"

"We're all responsible, Mom."

Turning loved ones into monsters is characteristic of people who have been hurt.

"I can't help you with this, Hermann. I have no solutions. And in any case what I see doesn't matter much anymore."

"That's too bad."

"What do you mean?"

"There are things I'll never be able to say to anyone else."

I sensed her breathing, closer.

"What things, Champ?"

"If you die, I won't be able to become somebody else. I mean, I won't really have any interest in becoming somebody else. If you don't see me … If parents don't see us anymore, it's not really interesting to go somewhere else. Who would we do it for?"

"For you, of course, Champ. For yourself." She was far away already, so far away. "Everything we are, what we become … There's something enduring in what people are to each other."

Would you do me the honour of visiting me one last time?

"Someone's expecting me, Mom. A friend. Not well at all."

"Then go, Hermann. Run, fly. What are you doing on the phone?"

35

I ran, yes. Alone like a solitary comet. The door, the park, the streets, the avenues, the stall, the vegetables, the building, Hu … I didn't run, I flew, with the thought that this wouldn't change anything in the grand scheme of ordinary life. While my blood was rushing in from everywhere and warming me, while my heart was beating as it never had before, tons of people were being born and dying. So? And then what? In the great history of the world, dinosaurs lived only eleven days and we, soft-shelled vertebrates if there ever were, have lived twelve minutes. It makes you humble.

I had to sit down for a moment to catch my breath. Bent double, my mouth filled with thick saliva that I swallowed as best I could. I knew the street yet I missed it twice, then found it again. I stopped right in front of the big house all stone and brick, the solitary fortress that resembled him like a sister.

⌇

The door, open again. Like yesterday. As always. Why lock a door that nobody knocks on? I crossed the threshold in silence after taking a deep breath to force my heart into more decorum and sobriety.

The house was silent, lit only by the slanting rays of the sun of this waning day. Where does one die most spontaneously? Of all the rooms in the house, which is the one you choose to end your days in? I thought first of the bedroom, you always think of it because of the comfort and the horizontal position that seem appropriate in such circumstances, but that wasn't like Hu. What was like him was the piano, the living room.

I went into the living room and called, "Sir?"

He was seated in the same armchair as the night before. I went over to him. He was sitting up very straight, his eyes half closed, his lips forming a half smile, unless it was the effect of the shadows. A sheet of paper lay on his knees.

I picked up the paper and sat down facing him. "Sir?"

I looked at him, it was my turn to look at him, my gaze operates when I'm no longer seen, that's the life I've chosen. I was not at home, I was the guest. His bookcase covered an entire wall of the huge living room, but they were his books. I thought it would be improper to poke around, and anyway, I didn't feel like it. So I continued looking at him, speaking all alone and probably gesticulating a bit. Had it not been for the darkness that gradually filled the room and the absence of the customary sounds, the tinkling of glasses, the crackling of a fire in the fireplace, we might have seemed like two old friends chatting, oblivious to everything, so interested in their conversation that they were cut off from the whole world.

My eyes surveyed his tilted face, his shoulders, his thorax. His legs formed a bizarre curve, his feet looked as if they had been buried under the chair like things that were in the way. My gaze moved back up to his face, the mass of hair, his eyes looking down at what? At his hands, the last focus of his attention. And I finally saw what I hadn't seen: his right hand was incomplete, I can't find any other word to describe that gaping hole where the index and middle fingers should have been. It was bleeding profusely, the blood staining the pants and spreading gradually.

The message was getting soft in my hand.

Dear friend whom I never called by name, I greet you once again and thank you for coming. I promised you I wouldn't go back to the port, I have kept my promise. In this whole business, I don't feel I have treated you with disrespect, I feel I did only what I had to do. With regard to my music, you were right. I knew right away, beyond the shadow of a doubt, that you preferred the works from my youth. It showed on your forehead, in your mouth, in your eyes — you have no idea how much they speak (and much more clearly than you!). The two interpretations were recorded at different times, the first at twenty-four, the third at twenty-nine. The second one is more recent and is indeed bad. No matter. I ask you to live in peace and to dispose of my body without performing all those learned operations that are your daily lot and in which you are a past master.

In case you are still concerned about integrity, the two fingers are stored in a safe place, I don't consider it useful to tell you where, an old hand like you is perfectly capable of finding them by yourself.

One last thing: what continues to fly, as you say, what endures when the body is failing, is illusion. Or hope, if you prefer. Nothing else. But I am grateful to you for thinking it could be the soul. No one ever talked to me about the soul, at any rate, not with that frankness that must make you seem suspect. This morning, I walked to your laboratory to leave the envelope. I waited there until you came out. You had that slightly absurd look, awkward yet assured, stocky, rather short, the charm of which I cannot explain. I went home with my head down, not looking at anyone. For reasons I myself don't grasp and that I no longer care to understand, I wanted your image to be the last one imprinted on my retina.

Above all, don't be angry with me.

When I lifted my head again — illusion? desire? pure madness? — I saw Hu's lips tense very slightly. I knelt in front of him. His eyes were still shining and his smile was really a smile. I shook his shoulder: "Sir!" Under the fabric, the flesh was warm. I sat down again across from him and I waited.

I waited, yes. I stayed where I was, waiting for death to take him and tear him away from where he no longer wished to be. To go from death to life is nothing. Barely a switching error, at worst a miracle. But to go from life to death … I waited, as I am, slow, imperfect, confused, desperately eager for anything that isn't apprehended through reason. To see it — that. I knew it would be great, as the man had been. "When I play, I am God." The body passes, but what it was endures, even stones leave traces, something floats in the atmosphere, the air we breathe, the fog over the city, it's him, it's still him.

In a few moments, I would become myself again, the familiar Hermann who would stay with Clotilde, welcome her two brats, chat with Mrs. de Valois, discuss things with Julian, forget Zita, make up with Alfred, embalm again like nobody else, and try, in a final burst of optimism, to make peace with the extraterrestrial by the name of Simone. In a few moments, I would come back to the land of the living.

That's the way it was, the present. That's the way it was, *my* present. My life suddenly appeared to me as a whole, all its complexity contained in a tiny snapshot you could contemplate at leisure. Forty-six years of existence had brought me here, to this heavy house with the seconds ticking by in silence, in front of these eyes of glass whose black barrier of eyelashes was slowly lowering, this envelope of flesh of which only the hand was still alive, this red flow that refused to dry up, this body from which was escaping ... what? I don't want to say it, I don't know how to say it, that secret impalpable entity that shines forth and that Hu was bestowing on me. Accept the present. I felt no remorse, only compassion for myself, for what I was doing. Everything was becoming strangely concrete, the seconds, the house, the hand ... For a moment, that mutilated hand symbolized everything I loved, everything it was humanly possible to love on this earth, very little, all in all, three or four people, a dawn breaking, a face, a shadow on the wall, an animal, certain words ... I stood up, I knelt in front of Hu a second time, I put my arms around him and placed my lips on his warm forehead and stammered, "That's enough for me, that's enough."

When dawn gave the window a rosy tinge, I got up and called the hospital to come pick up the body, expressly requesting that it be brought back to me once the usual formalities had been completed. Then I returned to the lab and opened *In Praise of the Small: The Greatness of Miniatures*.

I didn't need to read it all to understand that the small was Hu Senior himself and the 259 pages of emphatic praise were more about his own self than about miniatures. The book was divided into two parts. The first, "Learning," covered Hu's youth up to adulthood. The second, "Achievements," spoke of the breadth of his knowledge, described his successes, prizes, and honours, listed the articles and books he had published, and so on. The last chapters went up to the present, alluding to "an intense social life," but without elaborating (in my life, I witnessed no social life whatsoever in the building) and without naming anybody. One old lady "dabbled in painting," another performed culinary miracles, a third "was totally involved with environmentalism," and two real young people, one fake one (the Scout, I imagine) and "a middle-aged man, a friendly fellow who spoke in a peculiar way" (me, no doubt) "warmed with their cheer (*sic*!) an environment that, all in all, bore the mark of maturity." In short, we were essentially, taking all types and ages together, a group of passive and eager extras to whom Hu dispensed greetings, advice, and witticisms. I thought of the fears of my old lady friends, their embarrassment at the prospect of having their relationships revealed. Hu was a thousand miles from all that, not so much, it seemed to me, out of sensitivity or tact as because very little, basically, had counted for him.

I could never have written that, I would have written just about anything but that.

But all that was nothing compared to the beginning. It would be an understatement to say that Hu had taken a lot of care with it. Part One, "Learning," was illustrated with photographs. All of them without exception showed Hu (you might wonder how he had managed to find so many volunteers to take pictures of him): Hu at the age of ten, twenty, thirty, forty, Hu smiling at the camera, basking in the sun, proudly showing off a son ...

The first pictures were whole and showed people other than him, his parents, a woman, his wife no doubt, friends, a dog, a cat, the child. Further on, the photographs had been cropped to show only the father, increasingly blocking out, for unknown reasons, the places and people in his life. Hu's wife gradually disappeared, her physical integrity placed under severe strain. From one picture to the next, she lost pieces, half a head, a shoulder, an arm, and there soon remained only a foot, an elbow, a shadow, and then nothing. The same fate was reserved for the son, whose limbs were gradually shortened. Sometimes the upper part vanished and the child was totally beheaded, leaving visible only the body, the thick waist, the strong legs that were already becoming evident, the shoes like two scuttled boats. Sometimes you could see only the head, the image stopped at the base of the neck and you had the impression the photograph was doctored, with the head dropped randomly into an unrelated background. The effect sought by Hu was a complete failure. Instead of focusing on the centre of the picture, where Hu was smiling broadly holding a cat in his arms, the eye unfailingly fled to what was absent, to the decapitated or trunkless body, whose cumbersome weight was all the more obvious for the attempts to conceal it.

Would you do me the honour of visiting me one last time?

At four o'clock, they brought the body. "Death resulting from a hemorrhage subsequent to a wound inflicted to the right hand," the report said.

I prepared my instruments and said, "Don't be afraid, I'll only do what's absolutely necessary, and everything according to the customary procedures." "I'm not afraid."

When the operation was finished, I went back to his house to get a suit and recover the missing fingers. Dressing Hu took forever, there should have been four of me. Then I sewed the fingers back on. Except for the colour, which was different from that of his hand, and the swelling of the joint of the last phalanx, the reconstruction looked real enough. When I was putting the body back in the refrigerated drawer — that isn't essential but I always do it — I hesitated. I would have had to force the ankles in and that violence was the last thing I wanted to do to Hu's body. I left him there where he was, on the metal table. I covered his body with a sheet, except for his head.

I spent the night reading.

In the morning, I went and knocked on Hu Senior's door. His face paled, it seemed to me, when I asked him to come with me to the Icebox. The building was waking up. Around us, the familiar noises of the morning could already be heard. Mrs. Claire was taking a bath, you could hear the pipes gurgling and the bathtub overflowing, possibly. Mrs. Fitzback and Heels were going out for their morning walk. Probably mistaking my shoes for those of his mistress, the dog came and stuck his muzzle on my heels. I had to direct him back to Mrs. Fitzback.

"I was wondering when you were going to come," Hu said immediately.

Inside my skull, there was an expanding air bubble that absolutely prevented me from thinking.

"Do you prefer the pistol or the blade?" he asked.

"I would prefer that you come with me to my laboratory."

"Why? Because it will be quicker after one of us expires? But if you're the one who goes first, I won't know what to do. I haven't the slightest idea of how you prepare your corpses, my dear sir." And then he chortled. It gave me quite a shock, I had never seen him laugh. The exercise did not seem to demand a superhuman effort from his body: orbicularis, masseter, risorius, platysmas, everything worked fine.

"Come now."

He didn't bat an eyelash.

"Miss Clotilde knew."

"What are you talking about?"

"I warned her that my seed might still be active, but she didn't seem to take me seriously."

"I didn't come about that."

"Why, then?"

"Come."

Going out the door, he turned around. "I'm a simple man, you know. I take what life offers, I try to enjoy it as best I can and as long as possible. With all those centenarians around me and an undertaker who's just waiting for a moment of weakness on our part to get his claws into us, you have to admit that some days it's easy to give in to discouragement. I'm only eighty-nine years old," he added with a shrug, "and when a creature as comely as she is sad, like Miss Clotilde, passes before me, I have but one desire: to throw myself on her like a starving man on a crumb of bread."

"I see."

"No, you don't see, that's the problem. You're in love with the absolute, you're a dreamer. I'm not trying to offend you in any way, but in courting Miss Clotilde, I never had the feeling of betraying anyone, especially not you. Admit that's something to think about. Have you never thought of becoming a Cistercian monk, a hermit in the Gobi Desert, or a full-time astronaut?"

"With two children on my hands, I think that would be difficult."

"Two?" A stunned silence. "Are you certain there are two?"

"That's what she says."

He frowned. "I'm not in the habit of scattering myself like that."

Outside, the air was saturated with the special sweetness that heralds the end of summer. We walked in silence, I deliberately taking long strides, he trotting behind me with nervous little steps.

"I don't see where you're taking me, sir. I don't understand."

∿

I opened the door of the vestibule and led Hu to my laboratory. When he saw the body, he froze. Hu Junior looked like he was asleep, his broad face miraculously turned toward us. His head was bent to the side, as if he were waiting for us and bidding us welcome.

The father contemplated the son from a distance for a long time without uttering a word. Then he slowly walked over to the long table.

I watched the two of them, beset by conflicting thoughts. Hu was old, Hu was not old, Hu was responsible for this death, Hu was not responsible. This man lying here, this immense musician, as Mrs. de Valois had said, was the work of Hu, the best thing he had done. I thought of Clotilde, of Zita. Because of this little yellow man standing motionless across from me, my life was going to take a turn that I hadn't wished for.

Time passed. Hu still wasn't moving, but his eyes kept running up and down his son's body. With his torso stiff, his round head immobile – the movement of his eyes was the only sign of his awareness – he looked like dry wood, like a fragile little tree that had come to the end of its road but was eternally reborn from its ashes. An hour went by without our exchanging a single word.

"Sir …"

Hu jumped as if I had touched him. He gave a long sigh and shook his head. "It's still too much," he said simply. He gave me a look of pure panic before lowering his eyes to his son again. "I still don't know what to make of all this."

I would have liked to say, "Look at him, keep looking at him," but that would have seemed improper.

"All my efforts have been in vain. That's the way it is."

"What efforts?"

"Each one of us forms a certain idea of greatness. My son's was much too high. Like everything about him, for that matter. Too big, too abundant, too heavy, too present. How can a father be expected to deal with that honourably?"

He walked around the table and stood in front of me. His eyes narrowed until they were no more than two thin black lines.

"My son was a typhoon, you know? A kind of raw energy that knocked over everything in its path and could satisfy its hunger only by devouring your very substance."

He stared at me without blinking. Things had been said, he wouldn't take them back. Instinctively, I placed my hand on the body. Hu lowered his head.

"At a certain point, you have to get away. Unless you harbour suicidal intentions or ignore the most basic survival instinct, you have to take off or risk being sucked into the typhoon."

I saw Hu again, his endless flesh, his way of walking, of grabbing bread, food, cigarettes, and bringing them to his mouth.

"I feel I did everything to support him, you know? To make him accept his limits. He didn't want to listen."

"Evidence that maybe the limits did not exist," I replied. "Evidence that maybe you should have done the opposite."

"Meaning?"

"Get him to accept his talent. He worried about his shortcomings, did you know? He considered himself mediocre."

Hu said nothing for a moment. He went back to the other side of the table, his eyes continued their tireless examination, pausing on one detail or another, but finally taking in that thing that has no real name, a dead body; that is, a being dispossessed, forever deprived of its worldly assets. This was indeed the image presented by the sleeping son, crammed into the white shirt and black tailcoat, an outfit he surely would not have appreciated but that had seemed to me to be the most dignified. The seconds ticked by in silence, heavy with that presence weighing between him and me. The two of us were alpha and omega, the starting point and the end point. What should have been done? What had we failed to do? We had no answer, but the feeling of waste I had at this time must have been felt by Hu as well.

When I was about to pull the sheet up, Hu raised his arm to stop me. He reached out his hand and stroked his son's cheek for a long time.

"The world was too small for him," he whispered. He looked at me boldly, a sad smile on his lips. "I imagine that you loved him. That you think I'm responsible for everything. You haven't read my manuscript, I know."

"I skimmed it."

I handed him a bag containing his son's effects. He took it with surprising eagerness, opened it, and buried his face in the cooled-off clothes. Then he gave it back to me. I opened the metal drawer that should have contained Hu and put the package in it.

"And you didn't understand?"

"Understand what?"

"My … my journey, the most important thing in my life."

His head came to just above the drawer, as if it had been cut off and placed on it.

"What does it matter whether or not I understood?"

"But you were in it. You were in my book."

A friendly fellow who spoke in a peculiar way, yes.

"Not as much as with Mrs. de Valois," I made the mistake of adding. "She painted me."

"Do you like looking like a buffalo?"

"I actually saw a pond."

"Buffalo or pond, you have to agree the resemblance is far from striking. While in my work, there's no possibility of error, you're really there, you're immediately recognizable: a middle-aged undertaker, rather insipid, altruistic, unhealthily absent-minded, pathologically devoted, who has two cats …"

"One cat."

"… and a woman he obviously doesn't know what to do with."

"Summaries are inevitably reductive!" I didn't add anything. What was there to add?

Hu looked at his delicate hands, his manicured fingernails; I looked at them too.

"Is this the end?" he asked, suddenly worried. "There must be an end, here, in this place," he added, taking a breath.

"Yes, but it's not yours."

The door banged and Julian and Alfred burst into the vestibule laughing. They stopped short in front of my door and observed us for a moment without saying anything.

"Sorry for interrupting," said Alfred.

Their gaze moved from the little man standing to the big one superbly stretched out on the table, and tried visibly to make connections.

"I'll explain, Alfred ..."

"No need, we're used to it."

And for once you're not talking to yourself," added Julian, smiling at Hu.

I made the introductions, trying to make them sound plausible. Alfred and Julian didn't listen, they just nodded in unison while waiting to go on to something else.

"Coffee and croissants, okay with you?" Alfred suggested. "It's on the house!"

"What's the occasion?" I asked.

"May I remind you that it's this morning," Alfred sighed.

"What?"

"The interns ... they'll be here at ten o'clock."

A dull, arrhythmic rumbling rose in the room. Hu spun around toward the window, alarmed. "What's that? An airplane? An earthquake?"

"It's him," replied Julian, pointing to me with his chin. "He's like that. His heart acts up over nothing."

"Get him a chair," Hu suggested.

"No need," said Alfred.

"Have you looked at yourself?" asked Julian. "You look like death warmed over. Beside you, the gentleman looks like a teenager."

Hu didn't smile, but he liked that.

"He works nights," Alfred explained.

"Which completely messes up his life," Julian added.

"Especially his private life. And ours, of course."

The droning sound stopped, my heart calmed down a bit, and I thought, so, it's all starting again. This morning when I haven't slept a wink all night, when I'm not presentable or good-looking, this morning something is starting again.

Today I woke up in a very good mood when I heard Mrs. Fitzback calling her dog. I was happy because the world was as I had left it the night before, because no tornado had demolished our building, and because no terrorists had blown up Mrs. Fitzback. Or Mrs. Boisvert-Dufradel. Or Mrs. de Valois. Say what you will, with all the misfortunes that daily rain down on our planet, you have to be able to acknowledge the small pleasures when they come along. Mrs. Fitzback is not strictly speaking a small pleasure, nor even a big one, but she's part of the events that recur unvaryingly every day and that give continuity all its meaning.

Winter has returned. There have been some dead, some living, some in-between. That's life.

Mrs. Claire has left us. She died one cold night in November, the kind of frigid night when you wouldn't put a dog out. While the liquid element played a role in her demise, she did not strictly speaking drown, at least not in her bathtub. One fine evening, for no apparent reason, she took out a chaise longue and, wearing only her little checked dress that looks like a tablecloth, lay down on it. The cold took hold of her, the rain did the rest.

Last fall, Mrs. de Valois started painting again. "To paint the park," she said. "With its pond and fountain," she added mischievously, as if she were trying to please me. All this is confusing. Making an appointment with me for next spring, she felt she should show me her sketches. I didn't know what to say and I didn't know what to think of them, because, whatever way I looked at them, those sketches all looked like me. The infamous pond was shaped more or less like my face and the little stream of water trying to spring up could very well have been the cowlick I've had standing up on my head since I was little. It seems that certain artists constantly redo the same things, as if they can't get over them, as if, year in, year out, they keep being amazed by the same shapes, the same configurations, to the point of being unable to paint anything else. For Mrs. de Valois, it's the sphere. That's her shape. Whether she paints a pond, a sun, my face, a sheep, an ant, or a ladder, it will inevitably be round. I like spheres a lot, they're shapes that are complete in themselves, autarkic, they're self-sufficient and don't ask anything of anyone.

Clotilde gave birth to those twins of hers. Two boys, a big one and a little one. Twins, yes, but not in the least monozygotic, much less univitelline. The big one has black hair and almond eyes, the little one doesn't have a hair on his head except for a thin brush of chestnut that grows low on the nape of his neck, not to say down his back. The effect is rather unnerving. It's as if the scalp had missed its target and, not wanting to fall to the ground, latched on as best it could to the fragile dorsal protuberances. The doctor assures us that the hair will go back to his skull before long. Obviously, the two newborns don't look alike and my supposed secretory azoospermia secreted something after all. They appear to have been created together, two spermatozoa advancing side by side toward the ovum in an atmosphere of conviviality and peaceful coexistence.

Hu did not seem overly interested in his progeny and that's fine. Even the swarthy one with straight hair, Hu Junior in miniature, did not have the good fortune to hold his attention. Probably he too is already too massive; it seems history has repeated itself and Hu can sire only giants. Clotilde is managing very well with her dizygotic twins, the pale one and the dark one. The anomaly is second nature to her and makes her impervious to the trials and tribulations of life.

Me? Well, I keep going. I stay on this side of the mirror because this is where life is. Because it's here, and not elsewhere, that the world unspools the tenuous thread of its history and because it's here that the others are, my loves, my sons, my dead, this sovereign land that is ceaselessly assembling its atoms.

Caring for the dead gives you a taste for things that endure. Being happy without them isn't possible for me. I am Charon, son of Night. I load them on my back, I lay them down in my boat to take them across the river, man among men, to the utmost boundary of the living. If I should do only that, I will deserve to stay. Without me, there would be nothing left for them, not the touch of my fingers on their eyes, of my palm on their mouths.

I cannot die.

Acknowledgements

Thank you to Réal Ouellet for his penetrating and inventive reading. Thank you to Éditions Alto for their welcome, to Antoine Tanguay for his creativity and his intuitive understanding of the literary text. And thank you to Kevin Williams and Greg Gibson at Talonbooks for publishing this English translation.

Translators

PHYLLIS ARONOFF translates fiction, non-fiction, and poetry from French to English. *The Wanderer*, her translation of Régine Robin's *La Québécoite*, received a Jewish Literary Award for fiction. *The Great Peace of Montreal of 1701*, by Gilles Havard, co-translated with Howard Scott, won the Quebec Writers' Federation Translation Award. *A Slight Case of Fatigue*, by Stéphane Bourguignon, another co-translation with Howard Scott, was a finalist for the Governor General's Literary Award. Phyllis Aronoff is a past president of the Literary Translators' Association of Canada and currently represents translators on the Public Lending Right Commission of Canada.

HOWARD SCOTT is a Montreal literary translator who works with fiction, non-fiction, and poetry. His translations include works by Madeleine Gagnon, science-fiction writer Élisabeth Vonarburg, and Canada's Poet Laureate, Michel Pleau. Scott received the Governor General's Literary Award for his translation of Louky Bersianik's *The Euguelion*. *The Great Peace of Montreal of 1701*, by Gilles Havard, which he co-translated with Phyllis Aronoff, won the Quebec Writers' Federation Translation Award. *A Slight Case of Fatigue*, by Stéphane Bourguignon, another co-translation with Phyllis Aronoff, was a finalist for the Governor General's Literary Award. Howard Scott is a past president of the Literary Translators' Association of Canada.

Hélène Vachon

HÉLÈNE VACHON combines considerable talent with a passion for literature. In addition to working for twenty years in the Quebec Ministry of Culture and Communications in Quebec City, she has published four novels, a number of translations, articles, and presentations, and more than twenty works of children's literature. She was a finalist for the Governor General's Literary Award in 1996, 1998, and 2000; in 1996, she won the Alvine-Bélisle prize for children's literature in Quebec. In 2002, she won the Governor General's Literary Award for Children's Literature and the Mr. Christie Book Award for *L'oiseau de passage*, and she was a finalist for the Governor General's Literary Award for her first novel for adults, *La tête ailleurs*.